Horrible Henry and the Headless Ghost

Suddenly his mattress flew into the air and he crashed on to the floor.

"You!" he cried, and hurled himself at Lady Ann. He went right through her and banged into the wall.

"You've got a lovely bruise! It's coming up in a lump! Hurrah!" cheered Lady Ann.

"You think you're so clever!" roared Henry. "You think you can get the better of me, don't you? You think you can make me into what *you* want! A poncy little gentleman! Well, you can't. I'm me! I like being me! I'm not changing for you, not for anyone!"

Horrible Henry and the Headless Ghost

Kara May

Illustrated by John Farman

Hippo Books
Scholastic Publications Limited
London

Scholastic Publications Ltd.,
10 Earlham Street, London WC2H 9RX, UK

Scholastic Inc.,
730 Broadway, New York. NY 10003, USA

Scholastic Tab Publications Ltd.,
123 Newkirk Road, Richmond Hill,
Ontario L4C 3G5, Canada

Ashton Scholastic Pty Ltd.,
PO Box 579, Gosford, New South Wales,
Australia

Ashton Scholastic Ltd.,
165 Marua Road, Panmure, Auckland 6,
New Zealand

Made and printed by Cox & Wyman Ltd., Reading, Berks.

10 9 8 7 6 5 4 3 2 1

Contents

For Mary

Thoughts of a Ghost-writer

When she saw what I'd called her story, Lady Ann said:

"You can't call it *Horrible Henry and the Headless Ghost. I* should come first. *I'm* the most important."

"I know, Lady Ann," I said. "But somehow it sounds better this way."

"That's as may be, Jemima. But if I'd known you were going to put Henry's name first, I wouldn't have let you write my story. I'd have got someone else."

How I came to meet Lady Ann I'll tell you later. All you need to know now is that we did meet and she told me to write her story. I pointed out I'd never written for a ghost before, but she said that didn't matter.

"Any fool can be a ghost-writer, there's nothing to it. You listen to what I say and write it down. You can use your own words, all ghost-writers do. But mind you keep to the facts."

I promised that I would. She didn't seem like a ghost to fall out with.

So every night when the house was quiet and Mum and Dad thought I was asleep, I'd put on my bedside lamp and get the pen and paper from their hiding place – under my mattress. I didn't tell anyone what I was up to. Well, imagine going to school and saying, "I know a headless ghost. She comes to my room at night and gets me to write her story." Of course, if they'd seen her for themselves that would have been different. In fact, I suggested this once.

"I'll decide who sees me and who doesn't! You stick to ghost-writing!" was the reply.

I'd no idea why Lady Ann had chosen me in the first place, and I didn't like to ask. But of course it was a great honour and I learnt a lot about ghosts, such as how they talk. I'd often wondered about this. "As ghosts don't have any flesh, they won't have voice-boxes, so how do they talk?" I'd ask myself.

Well, I found out. They use a kind of

telepathy – they make themselves heard in your mind.

I hear Lady Ann's voice as clearly as I'd hear you. My mind starts working like a radio receiver that tunes into a wave-band used by ghosts. They decide who hears them, as well as who sees them. And I think–

"People don't want to know what you think!" snapped Lady Ann. "They want to read my story. It's a tale the world should know about. Be quiet and let them get on with it!"

So I will.

Here it is! Read on!

Jemima Bunberry,
Ghost-writer.

I
Lady Ann Loses her Head

Lady Ann is a ghost. She carries her head tucked underneath her arm. The reason for this is that when she was alive, her husband, Lord Albert, had her head chopped off.

Lady Ann lived long ago, when lords and ladies lived in castles with moats round them to keep out their enemies. The lords owned huge amounts of land. They also owned people who had no rights of their own and were called serfs.

Life as a serf was hard. You lived in a hut made of branches that leaked all winter and buzzed with flies all summer. You were always hungry because you had to give the food you slogged your guts out growing to your owner. He let you keep just enough to stop you from starving to death, so you could keep on doing his work for him.

It was no fun being a serf. And it was no fun

being a lady either. Ladies, like serfs, belonged to the lords, their fathers or their brothers. They didn't belong to themselves at all.

When she was thirteen, Lady Ann's father decided that she would marry Lord Albert. "He's rich and powerful. It's a good marriage," he said.

"Good for you. Not for me," said Lady Ann, who even at that age had a mind of her own. "I think he's a pig. He's got small eyes and he chews his food with his mouth open. It makes me feel sick just to look at him."

But although Lady Ann had a mind of her own, her father owned her and she had to do what he said. So she ended up marrying Lord Albert.

It was not a happy marriage.

Lady Ann and Lord Albert were always rowing. At first Albert thought, she'll calm down. She'll become like everyone else's wife and do what I tell her without answering back and throwing things about.

The fact was that Lady Ann was quite likely to throw whatever came to hand at Lord

Albert's head in the heat of an argument. She wasn't fussy what it was: a jug of ale, a cushion, a bowl of soup, or whatever. Fortunately for Lord Albert, she wasn't a good shot and she usually missed. But, more than once, Lord Albert had to scrape his dinner off his face where Lady Ann had thrown it.

Lady Ann did try to be a good wife. Once, for a whole week, she didn't answer back and she didn't throw anything. She walked around with her eyes cast meekly down. When Lord Albert asked her something, she said, "Yes, my lord, whatever you say, my lord."

She even let him win at checkers so as to make him happy.

But then the crunch came. Lord Albert pushed his luck too far when he told her to sew a tapestry of him hunting deer. "All the other wives sew tapestries of their husbands doing bold deeds. I want you to do the same."

She wouldn't have minded peeling potatoes or doing the washing. (Not that people did a lot of that in those days. They wore the same clothes for months, even years, without washing them. And they weren't too fussy about washing themselves either.) But she hated sewing, and Lord Albert knew it.

"I'm sorry, my lord," said Lady Ann, "but if you want a tapestry of yourself, you'll have to get someone else to do it."

"But I want *you* to do it," he insisted. "You're my wife."

"Tough," replied Lady Ann.

Lord Albert went red. He yelled: "You'll do as I say, my lady. If I want you to sew a tapestry with me on it, you'll sew it!"

Now it was Lady Ann who went red. She'd been meek and mild for a whole week, saying nothing but "Yes, my lord," and "No, my lord," – and instead of being grateful, there he was bellowing at her to do something he knew she loathed! Enough was enough. Lady Ann exploded.

"I will not sew your stupid tapestry, you great oaf! I won't! Won't! Won't!"

To make sure that Albert got the message, she picked up her plate of jugged hare – they were having dinner at the time – and launched it in his direction. It landed on his head.

"Jackpot!" cried Lady Ann, and collapsed with laughter, while her lord wiped jugged hare from his eyes.

Lady Ann thought Lord Albert had got what he deserved. But he didn't see it that way. "She's got to go!" he decided. "She has got to go!"

He didn't hang about. He acted quickly. The next morning he announced, "Someone has stolen my chest of gold."

The chest of gold was found under the floorboards in Lady Ann's bedroom.

She denied having stolen it. "I didn't, I swear I didn't. It wouldn't surprise me if you'd put it there yourself, Albert." That was just what he *had* done, but no one believed her.

Well, that was that.

Lady Ann was found guilty. She was sent to the block and had her head chopped off. That is how she became a ghost at a young and tender age and why she walks about with her head tucked underneath her arm.

But that's not the end of Lady Ann's story. It's just the beginning.

2
Lady Ann's Revenge

Becoming a ghost didn't cool Lady Ann's high spirits or her temper. So far as her husband was concerned, her feelings towards him were even more hostile. As he'd planted his gold in her bedroom, accused her before all the world of being a thief and had her head chopped off, this wasn't surprising.

Ghosts are rather like living people. But in two ways they are different. They don't need food and they have no sense of time. So Lady Ann wasn't sure how long she had spent in secret ghostly regions before she came back to sort out Lord Albert.

When she did come back to earth, however, there'd been a few changes. Lord Albert had married again. His new wife was called Griselda.

Griselda was highly satisfactory from Lord Albert's point of view. To begin with, she thought he was the best thing since sliced venison. She agreed with everything he said, especially that he was the most handsome, brave and interesting man in England, if not the world. She always laughed at his jokes. She sewed hundreds of tapestries of him doing bold deeds, such as hunting boar, catching fish and pouring boiling oil on his enemies when they tried to invade his castle. She never complained if he slopped around in the mornings in his nightgear and didn't bother to pull up his stockings or buckle his shoes, which was another of his habits Lady Ann was always complaining about.

"You're as ugly as the back of a two-wheeled chariot," Lady Ann would say. "You can't afford to look a slob as well!"

Griselda was not the only change Lady Ann found at the castle. There was also George. George was five years old. He was Griselda's and Lord Albert's son. He was neither like his mother nor like his father but somewhere in between them both, which added up to nothing much at all.

Lady Ann didn't greatly care for Griselda

nor did she think much of young George, but she bore no grudge against them. Lord Albert was a different matter. She was after his blood for the wrong he had done her.

One morning, Lord Albert and Griselda were having breakfast in the great hall. They sat at either end of the table, Lord Albert at the top, Griselda at the bottom. The table was so long they had to shout to talk to each other, and it was a long trek for the servants. (If they'd had roller-skates in those days, it certainly would have saved the servants a lot of foot-slog.)

Lady Ann sat herself on the arm of Lord Albert's chair. He picked up a chicken leg (which was what they ate for breakfast in those days), and was just about to take a bite when she grabbed it and flung it over his shoulder. Griselda, who was sitting with her eyes cast down, didn't notice what had happened.

Lord Albert looked round in a rage to see who'd dared nick his chicken leg. But all the servants were at Lady Griselda's end of the table. There was no one there who could have done it. Puzzled, he picked up another chicken leg. The same thing happened.

Lord Albert felt a tingle down his spine. Something odd was going on. Something very odd indeed! Suddenly, he felt a chill draught around his neck. A log fire blazed in the fireplace, but his bones seemed to freeze to their marrow.

"Hullo, Albert," whispered Lady Ann, making herself visible to him, though not to the servants or to Griselda.

Albert turned as white as a sheet. His heart leapt to his mouth. Here he was on a perfectly ordinary Monday morning having breakfast with his wife, and the next thing he knows, there's his ex-wife sitting beside him with her head tucked underneath her arm – a ghost! There was no doubt she was a ghost, for although she wore a long gown, her body wasn't real and he could see right through it.

"Enjoying your breakfast, Albert dear?" purred Lady Ann, picking up a piece of ham and offering it to him.

"AAAAAAAAAAH!" screamed Lord Albert, and fled from the table.

Lord Albert didn't dare tell anyone what

had happened. He knew they wouldn't have believed him. They'd have thought he was losing his marbles if he'd told them he'd seen a headless ghost. So he said, "A wasp stung me." And when Griselda asked, "Where, beloved?" he got very angry and growled, "Never you mind!"

Lady Ann would leave Albert in peace for a while. He'd begin to think, "I was dreaming. I was imagining things." Then she'd turn up again, haunting him once more.

There was no doubt that Lady Ann meant him no good. Lord Albert could see that being ghostified hadn't changed her, and there was no mistaking the evil gleam in her ghostly eyes. He got so desperate, he actually got down on his knees and begged for mercy.

"Please, please forgive me. I was a rotter. I'm sorry. I'll do anything to make it up to you," he whimpered, "only please, please go away."

Lady Ann seemed to consider this. "What'll you do for me?" she asked.

"I'll . . . I'll . . . er . . . er . . . um . . ."

For once Lord Albert was stumped for words. How do you make it up to someone when you've chopped their head off? Beheading is so thoroughly final.

"What . . . what are you going to do to me?" he quavered.

Lady Ann smiled. From that smile, Lord Albert knew that whatever she had in store for him he wasn't going to enjoy it.

As the weeks passed, Lord Albert grew pale and thin. His clothes hung loosely and his fat hung about him in loose folds of skin. His eyes grew sunken and his face pale.

The doctor was called in. He said, "Give him

leeches to clean out his blood."

So a servant was sent to a nearby bog to collect leeches.

The leeches were stuck all over Lord Albert. They sucked out his old blood so that fresh new blood could replace it. But all that happened was that he grew paler and paler.

"I can't understand it," said the doctor. "Leeches are the best cure I know. I give 'em for anything from ingrowing toe-nails to smallpox. They usually work a treat." He fingered his beard and muttered, "This is beyond medicine."

So Griselda sent for the wizard.

The wizard arrived with his long cloak wrapped about him and his wand wrapped in a blue silk handkerchief. He was tall and thin and had a faraway look in his eyes as if his mind was somewhere else.

Lord Albert turned to the wizard, imploring, "Help me, I beg you."

The wizard gazed at him long and hard. He couldn't see Lady Ann. But he felt a ghostly presence. He knew his magic powers were no match for a ghost.

"I can't interfere between you and the unseen powers," he said.

Lord Albert threw himself back on his pillow. "All is lost!" he cried. "No one can save me! I'm done for!"

Lady Ann was moved to pity. It wasn't nice to see a bold, boastful man turned into a gibbering wreck. And he *had* been her husband, even if a wicked one. She was just about to say, "All right, Albert, I'll leave you in peace. I've punished you enough," when he turned on her and said:

"You should have sewn that tapestry. If you'd been a good wife and done as you were told, I wouldn't have had your head chopped off. You made me do it. This is all your fault!"

Silence.

Lady Ann did not reply. It was the only time Lord Albert could remember that she hadn't answered him back. She simply vanished.

He felt an upsurge of his old self. I've got the better of her after all, he thought. When I told her where to get off, instead of being afraid of her, she couldn't take it. She scarpered!

Lord Albert began to recover. He started eating and was almost back to normal within a couple of weeks.

"Some fresh air might do you good, my angel," said Griselda one morning.

"I'll decide what's good for me, woman," retorted Lord Albert. He didn't want Griselda thinking he'd become a weakling.

However, the next day he sent for his horse. "I'm going hunting," he announced.

He kissed Griselda and patted young George on the head. "See you at supper, m' dears," he said. Then he rode off into the forest with his old servant John who'd known him since he was a baby and had loathed him ever since. (Not that he let Lord Albert know, of course.)

Lord Albert shot a few pigeons and a few crows. Then he saw a deer.

"My! He's a big chap! I'll bag him!"

He galloped off in pursuit of the fleeing deer, his eyes gleaming with excitement at the thought of the kill he'd make.

Then suddenly, there she was, right in front of him.

"Albert!" called Lady Ann.

Lord Albert shrieked, let go of the reins and fell from his horse. He fell on his head and was instantly killed.

Lady Ann wondered if she'd meet him as a ghost. She hoped not. And in fact, his funeral was the last she saw of him.

Lady Ann stayed around the castle because it had, after all, been her home and she was used to it. She made sure that no one saw her, though occasionally a servant might feel a strange icy blast pass him by or catch a glimpse of a gown that suddenly vanished.

What became of Griselda and young George?

Well, Lady Griselda spent all her time doing good works. She visited the serfs with bowls of soup when they were sick and let their childdren play in the orchard. She even let them pick the fruit. (Lord Albert always used to hang them if they took so much as a cherry.)

George grew into an ordinary boring young man with nothing special about him. When he was old enough he went off to fight in foreign lands, not because he really wanted to, but because all the other young men went and he didn't want to be the odd one out.

Lady Ann could have followed him. (Being a ghost she could travel anywhere without difficulty.) But she was bored with young George. She was also bored with Griselda. She was all in favour of good works. "But there's more to life than bowls of soup," said Lady Ann. "I'm fed up with the pair of them." So she took herself off to the ghostly regions once again.

"What did you do there?" I asked.

"Never you mind. Now get ready to start a new chapter."

"Are we coming to the bit about Henry?"

"Wait and see," said Lady Ann.

So I sat with my pen at the ready, and waited.

3
A Leap in Time

When Lady Ann had been in the ghostly regions for a while, her curiosity got the better of her. She couldn't resist coming back to earth to see what had happened to Griselda and George. They weren't blood relations but they were the only family she knew of, alive or dead. She thought a good few years had passed since she had last seen them. A few decades, perhaps.

"I expect Griselda will be old and grey and as wrinkled as a walnut. George, too, might have a few grey hairs. And probably a wife and children of his own."

But Griselda and George were gone without trace. Even worse, the castle had vanished. Not in her wildest imaginings had she expected that! But there, in its place, stood the tallest building Lady Ann had ever seen.

"The latest in cathedrals, I suppose! Well, I

don't think much of it. It doesn't make me
think of God, it puts me more in mind of the
devil. No wonder the nuns and monks look so
miserable," she thought, looking at the men
and women bent over their desks. "In my day,
the religious orders were a merry lot, always
smiling up to heaven, on the look-out for
angels!"

"The Barbarians!" shrieked Lady Ann with
a howl of rage and indignation. "They've cut
down the forests, my beautiful forests!"

Vast forests had once stretched about the

castle. Now in their place were bricks and mortar, glass and concrete. Houses and shops, office blocks and roads. All that remained of the forests was the occasional tree. Suddenly, it dawned on Lady Ann what had happened.

"More time has gone by than I thought!"

She was right! Hundreds of years had passed, not just a few decades.

Lady Ann wasn't in the slightest put out. To the contrary, she was bursting with curiosity as she set off to explore the town. She was thrilled to have unexpectedly found herself in the twentieth century. Not that she approved of everything.

"Thank goodness I'm a ghost, and don't have to breathe! That black stuff belching out of the back ends of motor cars would choke me to death in a week! On the other hand," she thought, "they've done away with the chamber pot. We had them ponging away all over the castle – in the dining hall, the bedroom, in every nook and cranny. The lavatory is an improvement, and I must say I'm impressed by the serfs – or rather the lack of them! There aren't any! Even the poorest wretches can live where they want and choose their own masters. And as for the women! My oh my!"

She saw women in charge of schools and hospitals. Women sitting in grand offices, bossing lots of men about. Women ticking their husbands off and telling them what to cook for dinner.

"Oh, if only I were alive today!" cried Lady Ann. "My father couldn't sell me off like a cow or sheep. I wouldn't have to marry Albert. I wouldn't have to marry anyone. I could get a job!" She fancied a job in government. "Telling people what taxes to pay and what wars to fight would be right up my street!"

But on a closer look, Lady Ann realized the picture wasn't quite as rosy as she'd thought. There were too many men like Albert, bullying big-wigs dishing out orders. And too many underlings jumping to carry them out. Too many rich lazy clods who had lots of everything. And too many hard workers who had little of anything.

"There aren't any serfs," thought Lady Ann. "But there are still plenty of drudges.

But things *are* better than they were. One has to look on the bright side."

Lady Ann was so busy exploring Castledown, as the town was called, that she forgot why she'd come back to earth in the first place. She forgot all about looking for Griselda and George, till one afternoon when she was taking a stroll (invisibly) down Cherry Tree Walk. Curiously, this was where the cherry orchard had been. She remembered that it had been a favourite spot of Griselda's.

"But of course, Griselda will have been ghostified long ago. And so will young George. They were all the family I had. What a shame I lost touch with them while they were alive–"

"Jumping Jezebel!" cried Lady Ann. "It's Albert!"

If she hadn't been a ghost, she would have fainted. As it was she stood rooted to the spot, staring at the figure walking towards her. It wasn't a ghost. Now she looked more closely she saw it wasn't even a man. It was a flesh and blood boy. Printed on the school book he was carrying was the name: HENRY.

"His name might be Henry, but he's the spitting image of Albert!"

There was no doubt in Lady Ann's mind. Dead or alive, she'd never been so sure of anything. The boy Henry had Albert's blood running in his veins.

"Albert must be his great-great grandfather! That makes me his sort of grandmother, thirty times removed!"

Lady Ann gazed rapturously at Henry. She had had no children of her own. Now hundreds of years of pent-up motherly feeling came bursting to the surface.

"My grandson!" she sighed. "What joy! What happiness!"

Lady Ann was bursting with love and pride. She hadn't been so excited since she'd had her head chopped off. And even that had been a very different kind of excitement. Now she felt like dancing with joy. She longed to fling her arms round Henry's neck and declare:

"I'm your long lost grandmother, thirty times removed."

But being a ghost, it wasn't quite as simple as that. And, besides, she didn't want to frighten him. Not that she thought Henry looked a fearful sort of child. She detected a bold glint in his eye and he walked with such a determined tread.

"He looks as if he'd take on the whole world without turning a hair, the little love!" purred Lady Ann.

But she decided a street was no place for a family reunion. She wouldn't introduce herself just yet.

"I shall wait till we're alone," thought Lady Ann. "Oh what fun it will be! What cosy little chats we'll have. I can't wait for us to get together! My own little grandson!"

Just what kind of a grandson Henry was, Lady Ann was about to discover!

4
Henry

As he made his way home from school, Henry had no idea that a headless ghost was floating invisibly above his head, gazing down at him with doting eyes. So far as he was concerned, it was just an ordinary boring day, not a day that would change his life forever. He mooched down Cherry Tree Walk with a scowl on his face and the corners of his mouth turned down.

"I wonder what's troubling him. Poor dear," thought Lady Ann, as Henry swung his school bag in the air and bashed a lamppost with it.

"I'm fed up!" he muttered. "That's what I am! Fed up!" He didn't know why, he just was. He took another bash at the lamppost, a harder one this time. His books went flying through the air and fell, scattered, to the ground. "Oh no!" cried Henry. "That's all I need!"

He was tempted to leave the books where they were, but they weren't all school books, one or two were his own. So grumbling fiercely to himself he bent to pick them up.

He'd just picked up the last one when he saw a large marmalade cat. It was sitting in the middle of the pavement before him. Henry glowered at it.

"What are you gawping at! Get outta my way, Fat Cat!"

The cat was well brushed and sleek. It looked as if it was used to being petted and spoiled, and certainly wasn't expecting what it got: the end of Henry's boot. It leapt aside just in time, and gave an indignant yowl.

"Serves you right," retorted Henry. "You shouldn't have been sitting there. Pavements are for people not cats."

From beside his left ear, Lady Ann nodded in agreement. Cats acted as if they owned the world. She had never got on with them and her Henry, it seemed, was just the same.

The afternoon was hot and filled with the delightful sounds of summer. Bees buzzed, birds warbled merrily and contented insects droned in the heat of the sun. Everyone looked happy. Everyone, that is, except Henry. He stomped at speed down Cherry Tree Walk, his eyes darting here and there on the lookout for trouble. He had his fists at the ready, just in case. "If anyone tries anything, this is what they'll get!"

WHAM!

He punched at the air with his fists.

THWACK!

He took a well-aimed kick at a dandelion head that peered up through the pavement. The flower head was knocked off its stalk. "I'll give it to Mum," thought Henry. "Mum likes flowers." But then he changed his mind. "No, I won't," he decided, "I'll keep it just for me."

Henry put the dandelion head in his pocket, and Lady Ann cooed with delight. She used to collect flowers too, and press them in a book. She and Henry had so much in common. "But can this be home?" she wondered as Henry kicked open the gate of number 27.

Henry kicked so hard the gate fell off its hinges. But he didn't seem to notice and thundered up the path and hammered on the door with his fists and then his feet.

"Let me in!" he bellowed. "It's me! Let me in."

"The poor mite must be desperate to get to the lavatory!" cried Lady Ann in concern. "At last! Here comes the maid." She sighed with relief on her grandson's account as the door was opened by a frail, wispy woman in a faded flowery dress.

"You took your time!" snorted Henry. "I've

got better things to do than spend all day on the doorstep!"

"I'm sorry," said the woman, flattening herself against the wall to let him pass. "But I was up a ladder putting in a light bulb. I was in such a hurry to let you in, I fell and cut my knee." To prove the point, she showed him the blood oozing down her leg.

Henry shrugged. "You should have looked where you were going. Anyway, I don't want to look at your blood. What I want is my tea."

"What would you like to eat?" the woman timidly enquired.

"You're always asking me that!" groaned Henry. "I'm not a cook, am I? Can't you think of anything for once?" Well, since he had to do all the thinking, he'd ask for as many things as he could think of.

"I'll have baked beans, sausages, chips, jam sandwiches, fish fingers, poppadoms, Coke and chocolate cake!" Grinning to himself, Henry flung himself in a chair and plonked his feet on the kitchen table.

"I'm glad to see Henry has a firm way with

servants," thought Lady Ann. In fact, now she came to think of it, Henry's maid had a strong likeness to one of the castle scivvies, an empty headed creature who jumped whenever you spoke to her. If she hadn't had her head chopped off, she'd have given the girl the sack. And unless Henry's maid improved her ways, she would tell him to do the same.

"But he seems to have the situation in hand," she thought, as Henry asked every two minutes how long it would be before his tea was ready.

"Now what!" he demanded, as the woman gave a startled little squawk.

She held out an empty cake tin. "The chocolate cake! It's gone!"

"Of course it's gone! I ate it!"

"What, *all* of it! But I only bought it yesterday."

Henry gave weary sigh. "*If* you remember, *if* you can remember anything for once, I had some for my tea and the rest later. I was hungry. You wouldn't want me to starve, would you?"

The woman hastened to assure him that she

wouldn't and asked if he fancied doughnuts instead, she had a full packet of doughnuts.

"I don't care if you've got a ton of doughnuts. I want chocolate cake!" roared Henry. "It's what I said and it's what I meant."

"Yes, dear, of course. I'll pop out and get you another one."

"And don't be long, Mum, I'm famished," said Henry.

Mum! Lady Ann's jaw dropped and her eyes popped in astonishment. The maid wasn't the maid. The maid was Henry's mother!

It took her some moments to get over the shock. But when she did, her first thought was for Henry. What a disappointment, what a misfortune for the boy to have that wishy-washy creature for his mother. But all the same, she was surprised by the way he treated her. In her day, it was the rule for wives to obey their husbands, but it was unheard of for mothers to obey their children. Not even Griselda would have stood for that!

"Times change, I suppose," mused Lady Ann. But it wasn't a change that she approved of. But she *did* approve of Henry's attitude to germs. She'd never been bothered by germs herself. Other people got the plague and smallpox, but not her. She told germs to keep away and they did.

"I'm not scared of a few germs," she was pleased to hear Henry say when his mum told him to wash his hands before tea. And to show that he meant it, he dug a piece of dirt from his thumb-nail, and swallowed it.

By the time he'd finished his tea, however, whether or not it was the germs, Henry wasn't feeling very well. His tea seemed to be whizzing round and round inside him. "My tummy feels like a concrete mixer," he muttered. But he wasn't going to be a wimp and let on to his mum. He just said he was going up to his room for a while. Maybe the food would settle down quicker if he was lying flat.

Henry stretched out on his bed and Lady Ann pulled up a chair and sat down beside him. She was just about to introduce herself and say, "I'm your beloved grandmother thirty times removed," when Henry jumped up. He was bored with lying down. He snatched up a pile of records and headed back downstairs.

"Mum, where are you? Come and listen to some records." His mum was in the sitting-room watching television.

"A television addict!" sniffed Lady Ann. "Watching one of those soppy soap operas, I dare say." But then she saw that she was mistaken. Henry's mum wasn't watching a soap opera. She was watching a programme called *How To Grow Turnips*.

"What are you watching that for?" asked Henry. "I don't like turnips."

"Neither do I, dear. But I do like gardening."

Henry looked puzzled. "But you never *do* any gardening."

"Well, no dear, there's no point really." His mum gave a wistful little sigh. "Whenever I try to grow anything either you trample on it or the slugs eat it. However, though I say it myself, I have green fingers when it comes to pot plants. And any gardening programme is a pleasure. It takes my mind off things."

Henry looked at his mum with interest. He

never knew what she was thinking and he was curious to know what went on inside her mind.

"What things, Mum?" he asked.

"Oh, just things," she replied.

Henry snorted in disgust. "What sort of answer's that! Anyway, I don't care. I'm going to listen to my records."

He switched off the television and his mum scuttled off to the kitchen, saying she had to do the washing up.

Henry sorted out his records and Lady Ann settled down on the sofa to listen. She wondered what Henry would put on first. Harp music perhaps? A church choir? Or maybe a romantic little waltz?

"My goodness! Whatever is it?"

Lady Ann leapt up with a startled cry. If she'd had any skin, she would have jumped straight out of it.

THUMP! THUMP!

The walls of the room shook as a hefty beat pumped through the speakers. It was Henry's favourite record by his favourite group. They were called Grisly George and the Groaning

Goatherds and the record was called *More Gore*. It wasn't in the top ten. But he'd made everyone in his class buy it, and one day it would be.

"Yeah! Yeah! Yeah! Yeah!" yelled Henry.

He turned the volume up to full blast and began to prance about, stamping his feet and slapping his thighs.

Lady Ann sat and watched and listened. She had never seen anyone dance like Henry and she had never heard music like George and his Goatherds. She wondered if it *was* music. But whatever it was, Henry liked it and she was sure she would get to like it too, once she was used to it.

But try as she might, Lady Ann couldn't work up any enthusiasm for *More Gore* or *Basha Banga Wallop* or any of her grandson's records. And as she looked at Henry, she couldn't help but wish he'd stop leaping about like a mad monkey, tuck in his T-shirt and wash off the chocolate icing dotted about his face.

"I expect he's had a hard day at school, and he's all wound up," she thought. "Any

44

moment now, he'll calm down, tidy himself up and be the little gentleman I know he really is. Oh what a mercy!" Lady Ann sighed with relief as Henry turned off the record player and turned on the television.

"Mum, come and watch! There's a horror film on," hollered Henry.

"Are you sure you want to watch it?" asked his mum, as she peered in round the door. "I don't think I will. It's all about ghosts."

"So what! I like ghost films. I like ghost films best of all."

Lady Ann's face glowed with happiness. Dear Henry! Bless him! He couldn't have said anything that pleased her more.

The film, however, was not quite what she had expected. It presented ghosts in a most unflattering light, and whenever one got exterminated by the blast of a newly invented laser gun, Henry cheered and shouted:

"Gotcha, Spook! Hurrah!"

"You missed a terrific film, Mum, you should have watched it," said Henry, as he climbed into bed.

"Perhaps next time, dear," said his mum.

"You always say that, but you never do! Ow!" Henry screamed at full throttle and his mum jumped back in alarm. "What is it, dear? What's the matter?"

"You tucked in the blankets too tight. I can't breathe," groaned Henry.

"Oh, I'm sorry, dear, is that better?"

Henry's reply was to suck on the bubblegum which had kept him company all evening and blow a bubble.

"Henry, you really shouldn't you know," said his mum.

"Now what are you on about? Hey, watch this. I'll blow a bigger one."

"I'd rather you didn't blow one at all. It's not a good idea to eat sweets at night after you've brushed your teeth."

"Sez who!" demanded Henry.

"Well . . .," began his mum. But the only person she could think of on the spur of the moment was the dentist on the telly.

Henry whooped with scornful laughter. "You don't believe what *he* says, do you! He's only trying to flog his rotten old toothpaste. In fact," he added triumphantly, "I wouldn't be surprised if it was using his toothpaste that makes your teeth fall out, not eating sweets!"

"No dear, I'm sure that's not true. And don't ask me why, my mind's all of a fog."

"Oh stop twittering, Mum, you're keeping me awake," yawned Henry, opening his mouth without covering it and giving her a good view of his tonsils.

"Good night then, sleep tight, dear," said his mum, and she tip-toed from the room, quietly shutting the door behind her.

Henry grinned. "Mum's a walkover, I can get the better of her any day of the week." To prove his point, he filled the gum with spittle and began to blow. It would be his biggest bubble yet!

Lady Ann stood beside the bed and watched as Henry puffed up his cheeks and blew and blew. The bubble grew larger and larger and his face grew redder and redder. The veins on his forehead stood up and his eyes bulged.

"He's a monster," she screeched. "The boy's a little monster!"

The words were out before she knew it. She hadn't meant to say it. She hadn't *wanted* to say it. But the bubble was the last straw and the words had just burst out of her. She knew that they were true, and she faced the awful truth head on.

"My grandson is a vile, disgusting little pig!"

All her fond hopes were shattered. What a fool she had been! Henry had Albert's blood in him, and even watered down by hundreds of years it was enough to make him a disgrace to the human race. Just look at him! There was a dirty smudge on his forehead, blobs of chocolate icing on his nose and streaks of burst bubble gum splattered all over his chin.

"That a great family should have come to this! Oh the shame of it! Something must be done! And fast!" cried Lady Ann.

It was no use hoping his mum would take Henry in hand, the woman was a nincompoop. And his father, whoever and wherever he was, couldn't be up to much either. No father worth his salt would put up with a son like Henry.

"If anyone's going to turn that little horror into a gentleman, it's me!" Lady Ann's eyes hardened. "No time like the present," she decided.

5
First Encounter

Henry lay back on his pillow. He had a decision to make. Should he keep his bubblegum in his mouth all night? Or should he take it out? He decided to take it out so it could get some air.

"It'll freshen it up for the morning," he thought, sticking the soggy grey lump on the wall by his bed.

Then, as was his habit, he thought about his day. He'd got the results of his English test and his maths test. He'd come top in both. He'd also jumped the longest long-jump.

"Not a bad day, I suppose," he thought, trying to reach the chocolate icing on his cheek with his tongue. "Some parents'd be proud to have a son like me. But not my mum, oh no!" He gave a savage scowl. "Did she ask about the English test? Or the maths test? Did she even ask what sort of day I'd had? No! Not her! She never does! She's too busy moping about."

He tried to remember when he'd last seen his mother smile but he couldn't.

"She's always moping about something or other," thought Henry. "I don't know what's the matter with her. I bet my dad wouldn't be like that. I bet he'd always be laughing and he'd ask me what I did every single day and he'd give me a pat on the back and say 'Well done, son!' every time I came top.

"Anyway, I don't care! What do I care!" Henry suddenly burst out. Then he screwed up his face and put out his tongue at no one in particular.

Just then Henry felt an icy wind on his face. He shivered.

"Mum must have left the window open too wide, silly thing."

He got up to check. But the window was open just a little at the top.

"That's odd," he muttered. "I must have imagined it."

He was about to get back into bed when another chilly blast caught him. He hadn't imagined that one!

Henry felt the hairs rising on the back of his neck. There was something in the room. Then he saw it, a figure in a long gown with its head tucked underneath its arm. It was surrounded in a haze of blue light. And it was coming straight towards him!

Henry screamed: "*Mum!*" But no sound came. The scream stuck in his throat.

"Hullo, Henry," said Lady Ann.

Henry felt his blood turn cold. He was shaking from head to toe.

"Mum!" he shrieked. "It's a ghost!"

But to his horror, once again, the scream stayed stuck. He tried to run. But his legs wouldn't move. He was rooted to the spot.

"He doesn't look so pleased with himself now!" thought Lady Ann.

It wasn't the meeting she'd hoped for, but she wasn't to blame for that and she looked with satisfaction at the quivering sight before her. It wouldn't take her long to lick Henry into shape. He'd do what she told him. He'd be too scared to disobey her.

She moved in a little closer till her head was

facing his.

"Do you know who I am?"

Henry suddenly found his feet and his lungs. He gave a bloodcurdling cry and bolted downstairs. He'd never been so glad to see his mum.

"M-m-mum!" he stammered, wild eyed and perspiring.

"What is it, dear? Whatever's the matter?"

"Mum, I'm scared!" blurted Henry.

Henry? Scared? She couldn't have heard him right. "What was that, Henry? What did you say you were?"

"Oh, never mind! The thing is I saw a ghost! It spoke to me. And it didn't have a head. At least it had a head, but it was tucked underneath its arm! What's so funny? What are you laughing at?"

"Hee hee!" tittered Henry's mum. "A headless ghost!"

"Shut up!" bawled Henry. "What's the matter with you? It's not funny!"

"Oh you can't trick me like that!" said his mum. "It's terribly funny. You know how cross you get if I don't laugh at your jokes. But

53

I'm laughing now! Hee hee hee!"

"I'm not joking!" raged Henry. "Do I look as if I'm joking! I really did see a headless ghost!"

With amazement, his mum realized he meant what he said.

"A headless ghost, dear! Really? How interesting!" She didn't believe in ghosts, but this didn't seem the time to tell him.

Henry felt like exploding. Interesting! That's not how he'd describe it!

"You don't believe me, do you?"

He saw his mum hesitate. She never told lies. She didn't believe in telling lies. But then, he could see, she didn't believe in ghosts either.

"Er . . . er . . . er . . ." was all she said.

"Don't you care that I've been haunted by a ghost?" screamed Henry. "Other mothers would! But not you! If you don't believe me, come and see for yourself!"

Henry made his mum go first. He followed her up to his room and she switched on the light. There was no ghost to be seen.

"It was there," said Henry. "It was just by

my bed. It's not there now, but it was. I saw it, Mum." However, he felt a little less certain. Perhaps he'd imagined it after all.

"Well, if it comes back, come and tell me," said his mum. "If you're frightened dear, I'll stay with you till you fall asleep."

"Course I'm not frightened," said Henry. "I was only kidding."

All the same, he was sorry when his mum took him at his word and went back downstairs. Looking nervously about him, he got back into bed. He got down under the covers, and pulled them up over his head.

"Henry!"

Henry sat up like a startled rabbit. There it was again!

"AAAAAAAAH!"

Screaming like a banshee, he leapt out of bed and trod on a bit of Lego.

"Ouch!" he yelped, and headed back downstairs.

"It's there again Mum! It's come back!"

"What has dear?"

"The ghost, stupid!"

Again, he insisted his mum went up to his room. Again, there was no ghost to be seen.

"Are you sure this isn't a joke, Henry?" asked his mum, with her mouth open ready to laugh if need be.

"You're no use! You don't believe anything! Anyway. I'm not sleeping here. You can make me a bed in the sitting-room. I'll sleep on the sofa."

His mum gave a bright little smile. There was a gardening programme on called *Manure and Mulching*, she was just about to watch it.

"We can watch it together, Henry love. It might calm you down and help you get to sleep."

Henry gawped in disbelief. He must have the only mum in the world who wanted to watch a programme about manure! But before he could explode, his mum had turned off the television.

"Sorry dear. I'd forgotten for a moment you weren't keen on gardening. Oh well, never mind." His mum gave an inward sigh. She'd always wondered what mulching was and now she would never know.

All night long Henry tossed and turned. The blankets fell off and he woke up feeling like an iceberg with a crick in its neck. But even worse, he felt a prize twit.

"What got into me last night?" he wondered. "A headless ghost! I must have been seeing things! It must have been all the food I ate. Mum shouldn't have let me eat so much, it's her fault," he muttered.

Remembering what a fool he must have looked, belting downstairs, and screaming his head off, didn't help his temper, and he stormed into the kitchen.

"Where's my breakfast!" he demanded.

"It's all ready dear," said his mum. "Bacon and crispy fried bread, your favourite. I thought it'd sweeten you up. I mean, cheer you up."

"I don't need cheering up. And I don't want bacon. Eat it yourself."

"But you must eat something. You can't go to school on an empty stomach."

"Who says I can't? The Queen or God or someone?"

"Well no . . ."

"There you are then. Stop talking rubbish. I don't want any breakfast, and I'm not having any! So!"

"Don't forget I'm going to the hairdresser's this afternoon," called his mum, as he strode off down the path. "I'll try not to be late, but if I am, the key's under the mat!"

"All right! Don't tell the whole world!" roared Henry. "Now I've got to go or I'll be late for school. I can't stop nattering to you all day."

"No, dear, of course you can't," muttered his mum.

Then she went indoors, and sat down at the kitchen table, forgetting to finish her breakfast, and staring into space.

6
Henry Cleans Up

Lady Ann watched Henry as he set off down the path. She was inwardly boiling with rage.

"The abomination! Just wait till I get my hands on him!"

She'd decided not to act last night, after all. She'd given Henry a good fright and it was only fair to give him the benefit of every doubt, and see if a night's sleep improved him. It hadn't. If anything, he was even more unappetising than the night before. Well, she'd soon change that! But she would wait till she got him on his own, and he didn't have his mum to run to.

Lady Ann's mind worked fast and she drew up a plan of action there and then. She couldn't put it into practice till the afternoon, so in the meantime, she hung about the house, watching Henry's mum do the housework. It took her an hour to make her bed as she kept stopping to gaze out of the window, with her mind lost in a dream.

"If she's got a job to do, why doesn't she just get on with it?" thought Lady Ann.

She couldn't stand the sight of Henry's mum (whose name, it appeared, was Alice) dithering about any longer. She used her ghostly powers to wash the dishes, hoover the carpet, clean the windows and polish the furniture. It was done in no time. Alice was in such a dream, however, that she didn't notice and did it all again.

"Croaking crickets, what a drippy dreamer she is!" cried Lady Ann. "One day I shall have to sort her out."

But that day would have to wait. For the moment she had enough on her plate, sorting out Henry.

At last the time came for Alice to go to the hairdresser's. She let two buses go past because people jumped in the queue in front of her. She'd probably have missed the third, but when a large man with an umbrella pushed his way in front of her, Lady Ann made herself visible to him. He got such a fright he fainted and Alice was able to take her rightful seat on the bus.

The hairdresser's was called *His 'n Hers*. Men and women sat side by side, having their hair done, much to Lady Ann's surprise. In her day ladies did that sort of thing in private and as for men, she wasn't sure they did it at all! She couldn't imagine Albert having his hair cut by a woman, then dyed in blond streaks.

"Progress is a very strange thing," she thought. "But now I must find a way to detain Alice."

A young girl with orange spiked hair and green circles painted round her eyes began washing Alice's hair. Inspiration struck Lady Ann. She had a sudden idea of what to do. Smiling to herself, she slipped out of the room and nipped down to the cellar. There she found what she was looking for: the fuse-box. As a ghost, she had the power to draw electricity out of the air and send it where she wanted. She directed a super charge of electrical energy at the fuse box. Everything electrical stopped working, including the hairdriers.

"Oh blast! Another power cut!" everyone groaned.

The electricity workers were on strike at the time, so they blamed it on them. If they'd had their wits about them, they'd have noticed the other shops had their lights on, but at first no one thought to check.

Lady Ann hurried back upstairs to find Alice fretting that she'd be late for Henry's tea.

"Oh dear! What shall I do!"

But not even Alice could face making a spectacle of herself, going home on the bus with her hair dripping wet. "I'll just have to hope the power cut won't last too long and I won't be too late home and Henry won't be too cross," she thought. But she cheered up when the girl with the orange spiked hair brought her a gardening magazine to read, and she sat back to enjoy it.

"Good! That's settled Alice! Now to see to Henry!" thought Lady Ann.

PHHT!

She whisked herself back to 27 Cherry Tree

Walk, just in time to find Henry arriving on the doorstep.

"Mum! Mum!"

No answer.

"Hmph!" snorted Henry. "She'd never dare to keep me waiting. She must still be at the hairdresser's."

He got the key from under the mat and went indoors.

As Lady Ann expected, Henry headed straight for the kitchen. He helped himself to a handful of biscuits, some jam tarts and a can of Coke. Then he went into the sitting-room and stretched out, putting his muddy boots on the sofa. He munched his way through the jam tarts, wiped his jammy fingers on a cushion, then took a swig of Coke.

"Urp!" burped Henry.

"Henry!" whispered Lady Ann.

Henry leapt up like a scalded cat. There she was again, the headless ghost!

"Cooe-ee!" called Lady Ann.

"Ahhh!" screamed Henry. "It's her!"

He fled from the room and headed for the front door.

"Oh no you don't!" said Lady Ann, blocking his way.

Henry tore back down the hall, upstairs and down, round and round the house. Wherever he went, Lady Ann was there before him. At last, helpless with exhaustion, he collapsed in a corner of his bedroom.

Lady Ann smiled extremely nastily from her head tucked underneath her arm.

"Now you're sitting comfortably, we're going to have a little chat, Henry."

"Errrrrrrrrrrr!" was all that Henry could blabber.

"Don't interrupt!" roared Lady Ann. "I do the talking. And for once, you little toad, you are going to listen!"

Lady Ann stalked up and down, sending out icy blasts that made Henry shiver with cold as well as fear.

"Now, first things first. My name is Lady Ann. I was married to your grandfather, thirty times removed. His name was Lord Albert. He was an utterly revolting man just as you are an utterly revolting little boy. It was he who had my head chopped off."

Henry's curiosity was stronger than his fear. "Why, what had you done?" he asked.

"Nothing!" said Lady Ann. "And hold your tongue. I told you not to interrupt. Now, I've been watching you, and I don't like what I've seen. You have no manners. You are rude and greedy. You're a dirty little scruff. That's enough to be getting on with. What I want to know is: what are you going to do about it?"

Henry began to open his mouth to reply, but Lady Ann was too quick for him.

"I'll tell you what you're going to do about it. You're going to mend your ways. You are going to be polite, considerate of others and respectful of your elders. You are going to keep yourself spick and span. In other words, you're going to be a gentleman. And I don't mean next week, next month, or next year. I mean *now*!"

"I don't want to be a gentleman," muttered Henry, making a determined effort not to be afraid.

"What!" screeched Lady Ann.

"I said I don't want to be a gentleman. I want to be just as I am. And what I am is none of your business."

"None of my business! I'm your grand-mother thirty times removed!" She glowered at Henry with such fierceness that Henry, despite himself, felt his heart quaking.

"She's going to kill me!" he thought.

"You've been watching too many horror films. Ghosts don't kill people, you stupid boy! It's against ghost law."

Henry gawped.

"How d'you know what I was thinking?"

"Never you mind. And let it be a warning. I'll know what you're thinking *and* what you're doing, whether you can see me or not! Now let's get started."

"Started on what?"

"You!" snapped Lady Ann. "I want you clean from head to toe before your mother gets home. Go on! Move!"

Henry moved, as slowly as he dared, to the bathroom. Lady Ann stood over him as he washed his face and hands, scrubbed his neck and nails, cleaned his ears and brushed his hair.

"Shoe-laces!" she commanded.

"What about them?" said Henry.

"Do them up. And tuck in your T-shirt!"

Henry hesitated. But then he felt an icy blast pierce him to the marrow.

"All right, give me a chance!"

"Your mother's back," said Lady Ann, as the key turned in the lock. "Now go downstairs and say 'hullo'. Nicely."

"Oh Henry," puffed his mum, who'd run all the way from the bus, "I'm so sorry I'm late. There was a power cut, you see. I got back as quickly as I could."

Indeed she had. Her hair was still wet and dripped down in rat's tails.

Henry couldn't see Lady Ann, but he felt her sending shivers down his spine.

"That's all right, Mum," he mumbled.

Alice looked at him in astonishment. She'd expected an explosion.

"I'll get your tea," she said. "What would you like?"

Again, another spine-chilling blast.

"Anything," muttered Henry.

After tea, he said he'd like to watch a film about pirates.

"If there's nothing else you'd like to watch, Mother dear," Lady Ann hissed into his ear.

"If there's nothing else you'd like to watch, Mother dear," repeated Henry, through tightly gritted teeth.

There was a programme coming up called *Your Garden In Summer*, but Alice didn't snatch the opportunity to watch it. She was in such a state of shock at Henry's offer, she let it pass. "What's happened to him?" she wondered. "Is he sickening for something?"

When the pirate film was over, Henry took himself to bed, saying he felt like an early night. After his mum had tucked him in and gone back downstairs, Lady Ann appeared before him.

"This is just the start," she said. "As you've begun, I shall expect you to go on."

"Look, I can't spend all my time washing and stuff," said Henry. "Anyway, there's no point. There I was so clean you could eat off me, and Mum didn't even notice! She didn't even watch her gardening programme when I said she could."

Lady Ann had to admit that this was so.

"But I don't propose to argue. Get to sleep. I've had as much of you as I can take for one day!"

A final icy blast – and she was gone!

7
The Battle Begins

After Lady Ann had gone, Henry didn't go to sleep. He lay awake for a long time, thinking. Thinking about Lady Ann.

"Who does she think she is, bossing me about? She's only a ghost. Why should I be scared of her? She can't be that clever. If she's so smart, how come she got her head chopped off?"

Henry's brow furrowed. "I shouldn't have done what she said. All that washing and crawling round Mum. I felt a real creep. I like being me. I like being horrible. And I'm going to go on being horrible, and there's nothing Lady Ann can do about it!"

Henry remembered the bubblegum he'd stuck on the wall the night before. He unstuck it, and put it into his mouth and blew a few bubbles. He was still blowing them when he dropped off to sleep.

The next morning he woke up feeling bright and cheerful. He dressed himself, deliberately not tying his shoe-laces and deliberately not tucking in his T-shirt.

"That's better," he thought. "I feel like me again."

Then he banged downstairs, yelled at his mum to get his breakfast, and set off for school.

Henry liked school. He really enjoyed it. The reasons for this were:

1. He found the school work easy. Some children had to slog their guts out to stay in the middle of the class. Henry came top with no effort at all.

2. He was good at sport. He was the best striker in the football team and the fastest bowler in the cricket team. He was also quite amazingly brilliant when it came to swimming, athletics, gym and karate. Henry was bad at sport in just one thing: losing. But then he made sure he didn't lose, by fair means or foul, he wasn't fussy.

3. The other children in his class were scared

of him. They were scared of his vicious tongue and his nippy fists.

"No one tells me what to do," thought Henry, as he barged into the cloakroom. "I'll show Lady Ann, I'll show her!"

The cloakroom was empty apart from one other boy. The boy's name was Simon Beavers. Simon Beavers was a weed, all knock-knees and sniffles. He was also unfortunate – he was always at the bottom of the class *and* he had problems at home.

Henry knew about Simon's problems. It was common knowledge that Simon's dad drank and beat him, and that his mother was always poorly and had trouble with her legs, so he had to do the shopping and the housework. He got no thanks for it. His dad never thanked anyone for anything and his mum was one of those sickly people who is always whining. No matter how hard Simon tried to do things to please her (and he tried very hard) she just moaned, moaned, moaned about her aches and pains.

"Simon's a sucker. I wouldn't put up with that, I can tell you!" thought Henry.

But even so, as he looked at Simon's face, all pale and hollow-eyed (he'd been up half the night doing the ironing) Henry felt a twinge of pity. But as soon as he felt it, he brushed it aside.

"Lady Ann'll think I've turned good, just because she told me to," he thought. "Well if she thinks that she's got another think coming!"

To prove his point, he barged into poor Simon. Simon's books went flying, and he bent to pick them up.

WHAM!

Henry booted his behind. "How about that, Lady Ann!" he muttered, as Simon fell to the floor, flat on his face.

Simon looked up at Henry like a frightened rabbit. Henry felt a sudden chilly blast. Was it Lady Ann? It could have been a draught, but he wasn't sure. Well, he wasn't taking any chances. He jeered at Simon.

"You know what you are? You're a snivelling, snotty idiot. What are you?" he demanded.

Simon knew what was expected.

"I'm a snivelling, snotty idiot!" he whispered and, gathering up his books, he scampered from the cloakroom. But in his haste, he'd left a book behind. Henry picked it up and looked inside. On the last page was Simon's attempt at last night's homework. "I'll tear it out!" thought Henry. Then he paused, and thought it over. "That'd be really mean. He'll get into awful trouble. Well, I can't help that!" Before he could change his mind, he tore the page out. Then he took the book into the classroom, and handed it to Simon.

"You left this behind."

"Oh thanks," breathed Simon, overcome by Henry's rare and unexpected kindness.

The class shuffled to their feet as Mr Mullins came in. He was the form teacher, and very tall and thin. He was neither too soft nor too strict but somewhere in the middle, and he loved being a teacher.

"Each child is a plant with its own precious blossom, and it's up to me to help it grow," was his motto.

"Good morning, good morning, good morning!" cried Mr Mullins (more commonly known as Beanpole) as he bounded into the classroom.

He called the register and the children handed in their homework. Beanpole wrote some sums on the board.

"Now you get your little brains round that lot," he said, "and I'll have a look at your homework."

Willing himself not to feel guilty for the trouble he'd lined up for poor Simon, Henry watched as Beanpole started marking the books. The first book he opened was Simon's.

"What's the meaning of this, Simon!" frowned Mr Mullins.

"W-what, sir?" stammered Simon, turning as pink as a prawn, and his heart sinking down to his stomach. He knew he'd got his homework all wrong. After doing all the ironing, he'd felt too tired to spend much time on homework. But he'd tried his best, and Beanpole said trying counted as much as getting it right.

Mr Mullins held up Simon's book. There, where his homework should have been, was the ragged edge of a torn-out page.

"Where's your homework, Simon?" Beanpole enquired.

"But I did it! It was there, sir!"

"Then you tore it out? As I've said before, to get your work wrong is one thing. To tear out the page is quite another."

"But I didn't tear it out. Honestly, sir . . ."

"Are you saying someone else tore it out, Simon?" asked Mr Mullins, sternly.

Simon was saying just that! But he was too scared of Henry to say so.

"No, sir," he mumbled.

"On second thoughts," went on Mr Mullins, "you tore it out yourself?"

"Yes, sir." Simon's voice dropped to a whisper. "Very sorry, sir."

He bent his head, as if expecting an axe to fall, as he waited for the telling off to come.

But a surprise awaited him. Mr Mullins spoke firmly, but his face was gentle with kindness, "If you have trouble with your homework, Simon, you don't need to tear it up. Just come and see me. All right?"

Simon let out a sigh of relief. He looked gratefully at Mr Mullins.

"Yes, sir. Thank you, sir."

Henry couldn't believe it. How had Simon got away with it! "I'd have got a real blasting if I'd done that!" he thought, quite forgetting that he *had* done it!

A chill wind brushed his face, and Henry shivered.

"Oh heck! It's her!"

Despite the bold scowl he put on his face, Henry found himself shaking like a leaf.

For a moment, Lady Ann said nothing. She just stood in front of him, staring at him with cold, angry eyes.

Henry waited for gasps of astonishment from the rest of the class. It wasn't every day a headless ghost turned up in the classroom! But to his surprise, none came and it was he who gasped as his red felt-tip pen went flying up into the air. He reached out to grab it. But too late! Too late to stop it drawing a picture of Mr Mullins all over his sums book. The drawing didn't flatter Mr Mullins! It made him look like a scarecrow on a bad day.

But Lady Ann hadn't finished. Before Henry could stop it, the pen drew a bubble over Mr Mullins' head that said, "SIR IS A TWIT!" Then it flew through the air and hit Mr Mullins on the ear.

Mr Mullins leapt up from his desk.

"Henry! How dare you, boy!" He strode across to Henry. And saw the drawing of himself.

"What's the meaning of this?" he barked.

"I didn't do it, sir. Honest, sir," protested Henry.

"And you didn't throw your pen at my ear?"

"No. No, sir!"

"The pen is yours. The drawing is in your book. And you say you didn't do it! Then who, might I ask, is the culprit?" enquired Mr Mullins, with something like a sneer.

Henry pointed to Lady Ann, who was standing above Mr Mullin's head. Mr Mullins looked up. The whole class looked up.

"Look, sir!" cried Henry. "There she is! She's got a long dress on and her head under her arm!"

"Her head under her arm!" exclaimed Mr Mullins in a voice full of disbelief.

"Yes, sir. Her husband chopped it off, sir!"

Mr Mullins turned to the rest of the class.

"Maybe there's something wrong with my eyes. But I can't see a lady hovering in the air with or without a head! Can anyone else!"

"No, sir!" chorused all the class, except Henry.

"But sir, she's there! You must be able to see her . . ." Suddenly the awful truth dawned. No one could see Lady Ann but him.

"It's not fair!" he yelled at her. "You threw my pen and drew on my book. Go on, own up, tell sir!"

"Tell him yourself!" tittered Lady Ann.

"There, sir, you heard what she said!" cried Henry, turning triumphantly to Mr Mullins.

"What who said?" asked Mr Mullins icily.

"Lady Ann!"

"And who, might I enquire, is Lady Ann?"

A hush fell upon the classroom. Every eye was fixed on Henry. For the first time in his life, Henry felt himself blushing.

"I'm waiting, Henry," said Mr Mullins.

"She's an, er . . ., ancestor of mine. From the Middle Ages, sir." He felt himself turning even redder, knowing it must sound like a load of rubbish.

"Go on, Henry," said Mr Mullins.

Henry's heart sank. He knew Mr Mullins was just leading him on so he'd look even more ridiculous.

"Well, er . . . she turned up in my room one night. Now she's turned up again here! Just so as to get me into trouble! She's an evil old bat, sir!"

The last words came jumping out before Henry could stop them, as he saw Lady Ann rolling round with laughter.

"Another of your little jokes, eh, Henry?" asked Mr Mullins in a tone that Henry didn't like at all.

"No, sir."

"Well, I'm not laughing. And neither is anyone else. You're wasting my time which is bad enough. You're wasting your fellow students' time which is worse. By way of apology, you will spend the morning, lunch and afternoon breaks cleaning up the classroom."

Henry made a last ditch stand for justice.

"That's not fair, sir. You're always going on about how we should be fair to each other. Well, you're not being fair to me, blaming me for something I didn't do."

"Enough!" snapped Mr Mullins. "When you've tidied the classroom, you can then tidy up the stock cupboard *and* the cloakrooms. I want them spotless even if it takes you a week – which it will."

Mr Mullins strode back to his desk. Henry was finally silenced. There was no point in saying anything more. He'd only make things worse.

It was bad enough having to miss his breaks doing cleaning. It was even worse having Lady Ann following him about, pointing out things that he'd missed and messing up things he'd already tidied.

"Clear off!" he yelled at her.

But Lady Ann only laughed.

Henry threw the blackboard duster at her. It went right through her, and she didn't even notice.

"Temper, temper, Henry!"

"Grrrrrrrrrh!" Henry growled to himself like a raging bear.

At last, Lady Ann took herself off.

"But I'll be back, Henry, dear. I promise. I'll be back."

It wasn't just a promise. It was also a threat!

8
The Battle Goes on

Henry wasn't in a good mood when he got home from school. In fact he was exploding with rage at the trouble Lady Ann had caused him. He hit the front door so hard with the knocker that he made a dent in it. He pushed his mum aside so roughly that she fell over. Without a word, he headed for the kitchen.

"Oh be careful with your feet, dear. I've just washed the floor," called his mum.

"So what?" replied Henry, deliberately wiping his muddy shoes on the floor, then sliding over it to the biscuit tin.

"Oh Henry, look what you've done! I spent ages washing that floor. Now I'll have to do it again."

"So what?" said Henry for the second time. He stuffed his pockets with biscuits and marched up to his bedroom.

He had planned to paint a picture of Lady

Ann on the wall. He was good at drawing, much better than she was, and he could make her look really hideous, even more hideous than she really was. But the thought of having to look at her ugly mug when he went to sleep put him off, so he decided to work on his model aeroplanes instead.

Henry sat down at his workbench by the window. Making aeroplanes was his hobby, and it always cheered him up when he felt miserable. Delicately made models, which he'd crafted and painted, were set out on a shelf that ran the length of one wall and he was extremely proud of them.

"I'll work on the Spitfire," he decided. "I feel like spitting fire when I think of *her*."

As he worked on the model, he began to feel better. It was going to be one of his best ones yet. Lady Ann couldn't make anything as good as this. Anyway, she wouldn't be able to see what she was doing with her head stuck under her arm.

"She looks like she's carrying a cabbage," he chuckled, as he sat back to admire his handiwork.

"Hey, what's that?" Henry whizzed round as something hit him on the back of the neck.

THWACK!

It was a Tiger-moth, one of his aeroplanes.

CRASH!

It landed on the floor. In splinters.

Henry felt the blood rush to his face. "Where are you! Come on out, I know it's you, you evil old spook!"

Lady Ann melted out of the air before him. "Here I am, Henry dear."

"Take that!" Henry picked up a cushion and hurled it at her.

"Missed!" cried Lady Ann. She snatched up the Spitfire and aimed it at his nose.

"Ouch!" cried Henry.

"Good shot!" cried Lady Ann.

"I'll get you, see if I don't!"

Henry ran round the room like a demented bee, trying to catch her and dodge the missiles she launched at him, his precious model aeroplanes.

At last, puffed out and weary, he threw himself on his bed. Strewn about him were bits of wood, all that remained of his beloved collection.

"You . . . you . . .," spluttered Henry, blinking back his tears so she wouldn't see them. "It took me ages to make them. Ages and ages."

"So what!" shrugged Lady Ann.

Henry picked up the nearest thing to hand and threw it at her. He realized too late, as it crashed to the floor, it was the short-wave radio he'd saved up for months to buy. He gave a howl of rage.

"Henry, my sweet," purred Lady Ann, "you may as well accept it sooner rather than later. When I said I intended to teach you to mend your ways, I meant business!"

"Just leave me alone!" retorted Henry. "You're a bully."

"And you, of course, are not! How you grew up to be you, I can't imagine. Well, having met your mother, maybe I can!"

"You leave her out of this!" said Henry.

"And as for your father, what he's thinking of is beyond me!"

"My dad's not thinking anything," said Henry. "I'm a one-parent family! So!"

"A one-parent family? And what's that when it's at home!"

"It means I've only got one parent of course! Don't you know anything?"

Henry dodged, too late to miss the record that hit him on the ear.

"Goodbye *More Gore*, and good riddance!" grinned Lady Ann. "Now about your father? Where is he? Did he leave your mother?"

"What are you on about? My dad's dead," said Henry.

"Oh!" said Lady Ann in surprise, she hadn't thought of that.

"He got run over by a bus, if you want to know," said Henry.

"I can't say I've met him in the ghostly regions," said Lady Ann. "How long has he been there?"

"Years. I was only one when it happened."

"Lucky you!" said Lady Ann.

He looked at her in amazement.

"Lucky!" he exploded. "You think I'm lucky! Well, you would," he added. "But no one else does, let me tell you. They're sorry for me!"

"I can't think why!" said Lady Ann. "As far as I'm concerned, fathers are not always a good thing. Mine most definitely wasn't! If my father had been ghostified when I was a babe in arms, my life would have been very different I can tell you!"

Henry was silent for a moment, a puzzled frown on his face.

"Your dad might have been a pig," he said at last. "But mine wasn't. Mum says he was great. Everyone says he was great! And if he was here, he wouldn't let you boss me around, I can tell you! Now clear off!"

Basha Banga Wallop hit the dust, or at least the ground.

"Now, talking of your mother," said Lady Ann. "The way you behave towards her is a disgrace. Get yourself downstairs and apologize to her, now, at once, for general rudeness and tramping mud across the floor. I notice," she continued, "that you have a rather fancy bike in the garage."

"You wouldn't break that!" cried Henry. But he saw from the look on her face that she would.

"All right, all right! I'll apologize!"

"That's more like it!"

Henry thumped down to the kitchen, with Lady Ann behind him.

"Sorry I was rude, Mum. Sorry about the floor."

Alice stared at Henry in amazement.

"Now," murmured Lady Ann, so Henry alone could hear, "fetch the dustpan and brush to clean up the mess in your room."

"But you made the mess, not me!" muttered back Henry.

"Remember your bike," thought back Lady Ann.

"Where's the dustpan and brush, Mum?" mumbled Henry.

"Are you going to do some housework?" His mum looked at him with wide, disbelieving eyes. "Are you feeling all right? I heard the girl down the road has just come down with chicken-pox."

"I haven't got chicken pox. I've had it. I remember because I was covered in spots and they itched like anything. Now where's the dustpan and brush?"

"Please!" said Lady Ann.

"Please," said Henry.

All that evening, Henry was a model of good behaviour. He sat through a gardening programme and had a bath and even cut his toe-nails. They'd got so long they made holes in his socks and his mum was always having to darn them.

Worn out by the effort of being good, but full of unexploded rage, Henry tumbled into bed, watched over by Lady Ann.

"Sleep well," said his mum, tucking in the blankets too tight as usual. Then, as she stood back she gave a gasp of surprise. "What's happened to your lovely aeroplanes?"

"I got fed up with them so I threw them away," said Henry.

"Oh well, you know best," said his mum. She'd given up understanding Henry's ways long ago. It was easier to agree with everything he said.

As soon as his mum had shut the door behind her, Lady Ann turned to Henry.

"I think we're getting somewhere," she said with a smug smile that drove Henry absolutely wild. He pulled his worst face at her, stretching his mouth with his fingers and putting out his tongue.

Suddenly his mattress flew into the air and he crashed on to the floor.

"You!" he cried, and hurled himself at Lady Ann. He went right through her and banged into the wall.

"Ouch! My head!"

"You've got a lovely bruise! It's coming up in a lump! Hurrah!" cheered Lady Ann.

"You think you're so clever!" roared Henry. "You think you can get the better of me, don't you? You think you can make me into what *you* want! A poncy little gentleman! Well, you can't. I'm me! I like being me! I'm not changing for you, not for anyone! Do what you like to me, I don't care! I shan't take any notice! So!"

Henry stood with his hands firmly on his hips, and scowled at Lady Ann.

"Are you quite sure you mean that, Henry dear?" she asked, with a chilling edge to her voice that would have sent a shiver down the spine of the boldest of men. But Henry did not flinch.

"I wouldn't have said it if I didn't mean it, would I!" he retorted.

Instantly, a jar of dirty old paint-water flew off his desk and poured over his head.

"Why you . . ." He was about to hurl himself at her, as he'd done before. But he stopped himself. He shut his raging anger tightly inside himself.

"Thank you so much, Lady Ann," he said with sickly sweet smile. "Now I won't have to wash my hair for another month."

He walked slowly over to a chair and picked up a towel, and began to dry his hair.

The towel whirled out of the window.

Again, Henry gave a sickly sweet smile. "Thank you so much, Lady Ann. You've saved me the bother of drying it. I'll go to bed with it wet."

He picked up a blanket, settled down on the mattress on the floor and began to snore.

"I know you're not really asleep," said Lady Ann. "Here's a final word of warning. When I fight a battle, I win — sooner or later."

With those words, she melted into the air.

9
Henry's Dirtiest Deed

"I won't give in! I won't!"

That was Henry's first thought when he woke up the next morning.

"I'll show her," he fumed. "I'll show her! Be a little goody-goody! Pah! Never! She can do what she likes! See if I care!" He took a vow that he would be as beastly as he possibly could. "I won't let up, not for a minute!"

He was as good as his word. One bad deed followed the next, but not one escaped Lady Ann, and she retaliated without mercy. Henry found his bike smashed against the garage wall and his fishing rod broken in pieces. He was always in trouble at school for things he hadn't done and for things which he had done, but which Lady Ann had undone. He couldn't listen to his records. She broke them. He couldn't watch television. When he turned it on, she blocked out the electricity. He even missed the inter-school cricket match because she'd made him miss the coach by spooking his bedroom door so he couldn't open it from the inside and his mum couldn't open it from the outside. By the time he'd shinned down the drainpipe (nearly breaking his ankle) it was too late.

"Well, I have to expect to suffer," thought Henry. "It's war."

He began to see himself as a hero, a soldier who was being tortured by the enemy but wasn't giving in.

"Do your worst, Lady Ann!" he yelled, after she'd busted his Walkman when he'd deliberately torn a leaf off his mum's favourite pot plant. "You can roast me alive, but I'll never surrender! Watch this!" He booted his football through the kitchen window.

SMASH!

Into the washing up bowl!

SPLASH!

"Oh Henry, look what you've done!" cried his mum, wiping the soapy water from her eyes.

"Oh stop fussing!" Henry shouted back.

"You abomination!" screeched Lady Ann.
"I'll . . . I'll . . ."

Lady Ann broke off. She'd run out of
punishments and besides, it was plain that no
matter what she did to him, Henry would grin
and bear it.

"I'm flummoxed," she thought. "The little
monster's got me flummoxed."

But then she remembered a saying her old
nanny had taught her: *When in doubt do nowt.*

"Well, I'm in doubt, so I'll do nowt,"
decided Lady Ann. "I'll watch and wait and
bide my time." Henry might have won the

battle, but sure as night followed day *she* would win the war!

"Hey, where are you going?" called Henry, as Lady Ann melted into the air.

But Lady Ann was gone.

"That's odd," he thought. She hadn't paid him back for breaking the window and splashing his mum. That wasn't like her. I expect she's thinking of something especially horrible to do to me, he decided.

But the day passed, then another, and another. And though he went on being as vile as he could, there was no sign of Lady Ann. She was up to something. He hardly dared hope she had gone for good. He remembered her telling him how she'd plotted her revenge on Lord Albert. She hadn't given up till he was dead.

Lady Ann had always denied that she'd killed his grandfather thirty times removed.

"I turn up for a chat with Albert and the next thing I know, he's fallen off his horse."

"I don't think!" muttered Henry. "She knew Grandad would get a fright and fall off. Well, she's not scaring me to death."

"I'm not scared of you! Come on out, you evil old bat."

He thought he felt an icy blast on his back and swung quickly round. But there was no sign of Lady Ann.

The weeks went by, and although Henry never missed a chance to do a bad deed (such as running down Cherry Tree Walk ringing all the doorbells), he had neither sight nor sound of his ghostly grandmother. But he still couldn't quite believe she had given in and gone back for ever to the ghostly regions. He'd better go on being as horrible as he could for a little while longer.

"I'm getting fed up with this," he thought one day, as he walked along the street. He liked being horrible *most* of the time. But not *all* of the time. It was hard work having to think of horrible things to do non-stop, without a break, morning, noon and night.

"The holidays are bad enough as it is," muttered Henry. The summer holidays had started and an empty afternoon loomed ahead. He had nothing to do and no one to play with. At school, he could make people play with him. But in the holidays it wasn't so easy.

"I hate the holidays. Anyway, I don't care," he burst out. Then suddenly his face brightened. He saw someone he knew. It was Simon Beavers.

"So this is where he lives!" thought Henry.

Simon was in the front garden. He was on his knees by a flower bed pulling up weeds.

Henry paused. He hadn't spoken to anyone all day, except his mum, but she didn't count. It wouldn't hurt to give his tongue some exercise and have a chat with Simon.

He cleared his throat and leaned over the fence. "Hi," he said.

Simon looked up and blinked in the sunlight.

"It's me," Henry went on. He wasn't used to making conversation and didn't quite know what to say. "What are you doing?" he ventured, at last.

Simon looked puzzled. What did Henry think he was doing? Cleaning the windows?

"Gardening," he mumbled.

"My mum likes gardening," said Henry.

"I don't," said Simon.

"Me neither. We could go to the park if you want."

Simon sighed. "I can't, I've got to do this."

"Well, I could give you a hand I suppose. Then we could go."

Simon's thin little face beamed. "Wow, thanks, Henry. Would you really!"

But before Henry could reply, Simon's dad came charging out of the house.

"Simon, what are you doing? I told you to do the garden, not waste time yacking with a mate! Look!" He pulled up a buttercup. "You missed this one! That comes of not keeping your mind on what you're doing. Well, perhaps this'll teach you!"

WHACK!

He gave Simon's face a slap.

"You horrible bully!" yelled Henry, pulling his gargoyle face.

"You clear off or it'll be your turn next!" snarled Mr Beavers.

Henry pulled another face, and went fuming down the street.

"He ought to be locked up, he ought! I

know what I'll do! It'll serve him right!"

He went to the supermarket and bought some marshmallows.

"I'll give them to Simon, I'll throw them over the fence when his dad isn't looking! I hope Simon scoffs the lot and doesn't give his dad even one!"

He headed back towards Simon's house. Then, he stopped in his tracks in amazement and horror. He'd been on the brink of doing a kind deed! He gobbled up the marshmallows there and then, on the spot.

"That was close! I nearly slipped up there!" he thought. "I'd better do something really evil to make up for it!" But what? He racked his brains.

"Never mind, I expect I'll think of something later. Right now I'll go and buy some bubblegum."

The sweet shop was owned by a man called Mr Pickles. Mr Pickles had bought the shop during the Second World War. He'd been incredibly brave and saved his mates from being blown up by a land mine. But sadly, as a result, he'd had a leg blown off. Afterwards, he'd been given a medal for his courage and a wooden leg to replace the one he'd lost.

"Hullo, Mr Pickles," said Henry, as he walked into the shop.

At the sight of Henry, Mr Pickles screwed up his face like a crab apple and scowled back from behind his beard. Henry had always suspected Mr Pickles didn't like him. Now, he was sure of it.

"Right, I'll show him," he thought. "If you're up there, Lady Ann, take a look at this!"

With a sweep of his arm, Henry knocked over a stand of crisps.

"Oops! You'd better pick them up, Whiskers, before someone treads on them. Like this!"

Henry stamped hard.

CRUNCH!

"You little thug!" cried Mr Pickles. He reached out a hand and grabbed for Henry's ear. Henry ducked and as he stood up, knocked his head on a shelf.

"Ho! Ho! Serves you right!" laughed Mr Pickles.

Just then, Henry saw an enormous box of toffees which had fallen to the floor when he'd bumped his head. His eyes glinted. He'd kill two birds with one stone. He'd get his own back on old Whiskers and find out once and for all if he'd won the war with Lady Ann.

He grabbed the toffees and headed for the door.

"Thanks, Whiskers. Catch me if you can!"

"Come back! You haven't paid." Mr Pickles limped to the door. But it was too late. Henry was off down the street, and there was no one else in sight. He had no witness to Henry's crime. There was nothing he could do.

"I hope you choke on them," cried Mr Pickles, shaking his fist at the quickly disappearing Henry.

Henry raced round the corner, and ran all the way to the park. Puffing with exhaustion, he flopped on to a seat. He held up the toffees and rattled them loudly.

"Look what I've got Lady Ann!"

Nothing happened.

"She'd never let me get away with this! Lady Ann must have surrendered! I've done it! I've won! Three cheers for me!" In a burst of victorious pride, he opened up the toffees and started guzzling.

"Now I've won and she's gone, I can do what I like! I don't have to be bad all the time. I only have to bad when I want to. I might even try being good for a change, just to see what it's like."

He took a half-chewed toffee out of his

mouth, looked at it, and put it back again and licked his sticky fingers.

And then he felt it! An icy blast! Henry's insides lurched with fear, but he gave a brazen shout. "I know you're there, you old bat! Come on out!"

Lady Ann loomed up before him. At the sight of her, Henry's newborn thoughts of goodness vanished. As for Lady Ann, she hadn't heard them, she was in too much of a fury.

"Thief! You despicable little thief! You should be hung, drawn and quartered and stewed in boiling oil! Stealing from a helpless old man!"

"Oh stop carrying on, it was only a box of toffees," said Henry.

"I lost my head for stealing nothing!"

"Yes, well, you're not as clever as me, are you?" sneered Henry, doing his best to keep his voice from shaking. He'd never seen her look so angry. Her body was glowing red with rage. But he wasn't backing down! He would fight her to the last.

"It's no good you going on about the toffees," he continued, "because there's nothing you can do about it. You can't make me take them back because I've eaten them. Unless, of course, you want me to sick them up!"

"You . . . you . . . you . . .!" Lady Ann was lost for words. There were no words to describe the awfulness of Henry. She gazed with burning eyes at her grandson thirty times removed. His gloating cheeky face was stuck about with strands of stolen toffee. His jaw was thrust out with a boldness too much to bear.

"What can I do?" she wondered. "What can I do to punish him?" But try as she might, she could think of no punishment worthy of Henry's rudeness or his crime. She floundered about in a turmoil of despair. She was beaten, and she knew it.

If ghosts could weep, she would have wept.

A Chat with Lady Ann

When I'd finished writing the last chapter, *Henry's Dirtiest Deed*, I stretched and flexed my fingers.

"I've got writer's cramp, Lady Ann," I said.

"Are you complaining Jemima?"

I quickly assured her that I wasn't.

"That's all right then. Because if you are, I'll get myself another ghost-writer."

I begged her not to think of it.

After I've done my stint of ghost-writing, Lady Ann usually takes herself off. But sometimes she stays for a chat. I was particularly glad to have a chat that night, because there was something I wanted to talk to her about. Something that I'd been wondering about for a long time.

Henry was an example of something I'd often thought: if you're really wicked, you can get away with anything, but if you're good, it gets you nowhere.

It always seems to me it's the people who are good and kind and gentle who always get the worst of it. They're the ones who get terrible diseases and suffer catastrophes and have a generally dismal time. But people like Henry, who are mean and selfish, just go sailing along, having all the fun and the best of everything.

"In other words, Lady Ann," I said, "goodness just doesn't pay."

"You strange child! Whatever makes you think that?"

"Life," I sighed. "I mean look at you. You got your head chopped off because of Lord Albert's wickedness, not yours."

Now I came to the question I was burning to ask: "What I want to know is this: do people who've got away with being bad as humans get punished for it as ghosts?"

I didn't get the answer that I'd hoped for. In fact, I didn't get an answer at all!

"Never you mind," said Lady Ann. "Wait till you're a ghost, then you'll find out for yourself. Besides," she added, "who said Henry got away with it?"

"You mean you got him after all! Oh good!"
I cried. "What did you do to him?"

"I didn't do anything. Bad luck did it for
me. But I'll tell you about it tomorrow."

"Oh no! Please," I begged, "please tell me
now!"

I sat with my pen at the ready.

"You really should get to sleep. But just this
once, Jemima, very well. Start a new chapter,
and call it *Henry In Trouble*.

Then Lady Ann began . . .

10
Henry in Trouble

Bad luck struck Henry the very day after he'd stolen the toffees from Mr Pickles. He was coming back from the park when a car pulled to a screeching halt beside him. Two men leapt out and the next thing Henry knew, he was in the back of the car. A needle jabbed his arm.

"Helppppp . . ." Henry's voice faded into nothing as he lost consciousness.

When he came to, he was sitting bound and gagged in what looked like the belfry of a church. His first thought was: I've been kidnapped!

His mind was buzzing with questions: Why should anyone want to kidnap him? How long had he been there? Hours? Days? Months? He thought it was probably hours. If it had been longer, he'd have felt hungrier. As it was, he just felt a bit sick.

"It's the drug they gave me, I expect. Whoever *they* are!" thought Henry.

A host of dark thoughts rushed to his mind. He remembered reading in a newspaper about kidnappers who'd cut a boy's ear off.

"I've got to get out of here before *they* come back!"

He looked round for a means of escape. But the belfry had no door.

"How did they get me here?" he wondered.

Then he saw a handle on the floor. He bottom-bumped towards it and tried to lift it with his foot. No luck! It was bolted. Bolted from the outside. The walls looked a foot thick. And the windows were high up. Just narrow slits. Not even his shadow could squeeze through them.

Panic rose in Henry like a wave. Now what should he do? Call for help! he decided.

But first he had to remove the gag. It was tightly tied, but by rubbing the back of his head against the wall, he was able to loosen it so it fell away from his mouth.

"Help!" he cried, with his lungs at full throttle. "Help! Help!"

The only reply was the twittering of birds. "I must be in the country," he thought. "But someone's sure to come soon to say their prayers and sing hymns and stuff."

Henry's eyes lit up.

Church! Belfry! Bells!

"All I have to do is ring the bells! That'll bring people running!"

He looked up. No ropes! No bells! Just holes in the roof and cobwebs everywhere. The realization dawned: no one had been there for yonks – except for the kidnappers.

The awfulness of his situation hit savagely home. Fear gripped Henry like a giant hand. With the greatest of effort he willed himself not to have hysterics.

"I've got to keep calm! It's my only hope!"

The first thing was to have a careful look round. It was what people did in films when they were put in prisons. They looked round carefully for anything that might help them to escape.

Henry surveyed the belfry. His search was rewarded. In a shadowy corner he saw a pile of boxes. He edged his way towards them, and shouted with joy. In one box were some blankets. In the other was: food! Crisps, peanuts, chocolate, biscuits and a few cans of drink. At least the crooks had good taste in food!

He leaned across to get a packet of biscuits and opened them with his teeth. It wasn't easy but he managed it, and soon he'd scoffed the lot.

"Now I've got my strength up, I'll see if I can get these ropes off. They're cutting into me like anything," he muttered.

Henry looked round for something with a sharp edge, but without success. There was nothing else for it — he set to with his teeth. Luckily, his hands were tied at the front. He chewed at the ropes round his hands, spitting out the hairy tufts as he went.

At last the ropes frayed. Henry pulled and they snapped. His hands were free. Now, for his feet. It didn't take him long to untie them, and Henry leapt up in triumph.

"I'm free!" he shouted. "I'm free!"

Yes, free to run around the belfry! But that was as far as his freedom went. He was no nearer than before to escaping. Even so, after a can of Coke and a bar of chocolate, he felt better.

"The crooks will be back soon. They'll have realized by now they've got the wrong person. They must have thought I was someone else, someone with rich parents. Anyway, Mum'll have told the police I'm missing when I didn't get back for tea."

He paced about the belfry. Time passed. The light was fading. He became aware of something: something fluttering in the rafters.

BATS!

And something scuttling over the floor.

RATS!

Henry's courage failed him. He fainted right away.

The night was torture. He had nightmares when he was asleep. He dreamt he was being eaten by rats. His screams woke him up. And he found a real-life rat, there on the floor beside him.

"Someone must come soon!" he jabbered. "Even the crooks would be better than no one!"

But no, perhaps not.

"When they find out I'm not who they thought I was, they might go bananas and kill me!"

At last daylight came. It brought some relief, but not much, and Henry gave in to despair. Waves of self-pity swept over him. He had never felt sorry for anyone before in his life. Not even himself! He had always prided himself on being as tough as nails. But now he sat whimpering and wailing, a picture of misery. The day dragged by. All too soon it was dark again and he heard the dreaded fluttering and scuttling.

"I'll make a noise!" he thought desperately.

"I'll scare them off!"

He began to sing. Or rather bellow. He bellowed out *Grisly George*'s latest hit, *Get Outta My Way*:

Get outta my way
Get outta my way
I'm boss around here
So you do what I say
I got a fist like a hammer
I'm a thick moron
I like causing bovver
With me Doctor Martin's on
I ain't a pretty picture
I'm an 'orrible sight
When I look in the mirror
I give meself a fright!
Get outta my way!
Get outta my way!
Get outta my way!

To his dismay, Henry found the song wasn't having the effect that he'd hoped. Far from scaring off the rats and bats, they seemed to enjoy it. Even more of them came fluttering and scuttling about him waiting for an encore!

"This can't be happening! It's got to be a

dream! In a moment I'll wake up. Please let it be a dream! Please!" Henry babbled into the belfry.

A chill blast on his neck made him shiver. Henry swung round.

It was Lady Ann.

11

Bad News

Henry never thought he'd be glad to see Lady Ann. But when he saw her headless figure standing there beside him, he was overjoyed.

"Thank goodness you've found me. I've been kidnapped."

"I know," said Lady Ann, as if it was the most normal thing in the world. "I saw it happen!"

Henry was outraged. "You saw it? You let me get kidnapped?"

"What could I do about it?"

"You could have scared them off for one thing!"

"I suppose I could have. But I didn't want to," said Lady Ann. "I don't owe you any favours that I recall. As far as I'm concerned, a ratty, batty belfry is just the place for you."

"You're wicked!" screamed Henry. "That's what you are!"

"Temper! Temper! Henry!" warned Lady Ann. "Oh dear," she added, as she floated about the belfry, "not many home comforts here, are there?"

"I won't be here much longer," retorted Henry. "Someone'll find me."

"That's what you think," said Lady Ann with a cheerfulness that Henry didn't like. "Now pin back your ears, and I'll tell you who kidnapped you and why."

NOTE
It took Lady Ann most of the of the night to bring Henry up-to-date on his situation. He was only too glad to listen and, besides, it took his mind off the rats and bats. However, I have to be up early in the morning as I've got to go jogging. I'm going in for the school marathon. (Not wanting to boast, I think I'll probably win.) So I beg you to excuse me if just this once I summarize what Lady Ann told me as briefly as I can.
Jemima Bunberry

Names of kidnappers
Sid Jones and **Charlie Ferry**

Nicknames

Bone-Breaker   Chuck the Knife

Size

Gorilla-like   Ox-like

Age

18½   18¼

Job

Crook   Crook

Reason for kidnap

Money   Money

Person they meant to kidnap

Oliver Gooch, son of multi-millionare Joe Gooch. Only they kidnapped Henry by mistake.

What happened after Sid and Charlie put Henry in the belfry?

1. They went home to their pongy flat next to the gasworks.
2. They phoned Mr Gooch at his office on the 24th floor of a building in the City of London.
3. Mr Gooch answered the phone.

The phone call took place as follows:

MR GOOCH: Who's that?

SID: Never you mind who I am. All you need to know is we've got your son, Oliver.

MR GOOCH: (*pale as a sheet*) Oliver?

SID: Me and my mate kidnapped him. If you want to see him again, it'll cost you £1,000,000.

MR GOOCH: (*flabbergasted*) A million pounds?

SID: I'll phone you tonight to tell you where to put the money.

MR GOOCH: But I haven't got a million pounds! I —

SID: You'd better find it, Mister. Because if you don't, your young Ollie is a dodo.

MR GOOCH: (*not understanding*) A dodo?

SID: A goner, in plain English.

MR GOOCH: (*still not understanding*) A goner?

SID: A corpse, Dumbo. And don't be a silly-billy, will yer? Don't do anything stoopid, like telling the fuzz.

MR GOOCH: I don't know any fuzz.

SID: I mean the cops. Got it?

MR GOOCH: Oh, the police. Yes, I've got it.

SID: Good.

(Sid hangs up)

CHARLIE: You told him, Bone-Breaker.

SID: Yeah, I told him, Chuck. Soon you and me is gonna be very happy —

CHARLIE: Because we're going to be very—

TOGETHER: Rich! Ha ha ha ha!

But, back at Mr Gooch's office, as soon as Sid had rung off, Oliver walked in.

MR GOOCH: *(almost having a heart-attack)* Oliver, it's you!

OLIVER: Well, it's not my shadow. Come on, Dad, you promised to take me to buy a computer.

MR GOOCH: But a man just rang up and said you'd been kidnapped.

OLIVER: Well, I haven't. They must have got someone else by mistake.

MR GOOCH: Something fishy's going on. The computer will have to wait. I'm phoning the police.

The outcome of this was that the police were waiting when Sid phoned again. What Sid didn't know was that the line was bugged and the call was being traced.

SID: Is that you, Goochie?

MR GOOCH: Yes.

SID: You didn't go to the police, did yer?

MR GOOCH: No, no, of course not.

SID: Good, now about the money.

MR GOOCH: I'll have it by this time tomorrow.

SID: That's a good boy. Now, I'll tell you where to leave it.

Mr Gooch made himself out to be a bit thick and pretended he couldn't understand the instructions Sid was giving him. Sid had to go over everything ten times which took ages.

At last, Sid hung up.

SID: I told him, Chuck.

CHARLIE: You told him, Bone-Breaker. All we have to do now is pick up the money. Then we'll be—

BOTH: Millionaires! Ha ha ha!
(*Bang! Bang! Crash!*)

BOTH: Who's that!

POLICE: (*entering*) The police! Come along, you two, the game's up.

The next morning, Sid and Charlie found themselves in court, up before the judge.

SID: We was only joking, your Honour.

CHARLIE: Just our little joke, see.

SID: We wouldn't kidnap a kid, would we Chuck?

CHARLIE: Course we wouldn't Bone-Breaker. We love children. We was children ourselves once.

JUDGE: Quiet!

SID: Just one more word, pleasing Your Honour.

JUDGE: Oh, very well. Get on with it.

SID: The proof that we was only joking when we said we'd kidnapped his Oliver, is that we didn't kidnap him.

CHARLIE: Like we said, Your Honour, it was just a joke.

JUDGE: Just a joke, eh? Well, I don't think it's funny. Prison for 28 days!
          (*Sid and Charlie are taken to their cell.*)

SID: Phew, that was lucky. If the Judge had known we'd really kidnapped someone, we'd have got 28 *years*, not 28 days!

CHARLIE: I wonder who he was?

SID: The kid? I dunno. Still, no point in thinking about him.

CHARLIE: No, we got problems of our own. Best not think about him.

SID: Yeah, you're right, Chuck. Least said, soonest mended.

"What's that supposed to mean?" cried Henry, who had listened to the account of his kidnappers with increasing dismay.

"It means the less they think of you, the better it is for them!" said Lady Ann.

"But those crooks can't just leave me here!"

"Why not?" asked Lady Ann.

"No one else knows where I am! I'll starve. I've hardly any food left."

"To be accurate, you've *no* food left. You've just scoffed the last biscuit."

"I was hungry!" said Henry.

"Well, you'll be even hungrier now won't you?" said Lady Ann. "Still, no use crying over spilt milk. Or should I say, eaten biscuits? I suppose the sooner it's all over the better."

"The sooner what's over?" demanded Henry.

"Why, you of course. Your human life, at any rate. You've all eternity as a ghost. You may as well die of starvation as anything else."

"You're not going to let me die!" raged Henry.

"I intend to do precisely that. You're a menace. No good to anyone. Good riddance to bad rubbish say I!"

"I hate you!" screamed Henry. "It's not fair! Why can't I have a nice Grandma like other children? A proper Grandma with a head!"

Lady Ann gave Henry a glowering glance.

"Sticks and stones don't hurt me, Henry. And your words most certainly don't."

Henry stamped his foot. "Look you, I've had enough messing around. You get me out of here. I'm a kidnapped child. It's your duty to save me!"

"Why?" asked Lady Ann.

"Stop asking 'why' all the time! Because you should, that's why!"

"Who have you ever helped, Henry dear?" asked Lady Ann in the oh-so-sweet voice Henry found absolutely maddening.

"This is different! This is life and death!"

Lady Ann was unmoved. She just shrugged.

"I get your game!" snarled Henry. "You want me down on my knees, begging you to help me! 'Please save me, Lady Ann. I'll be a good little boy, Lady Ann.' That's what you want, isn't it?"

"Right!" said Lady Ann. "And this, I warn you, is your last chance. You promise to mend your ways or, as Sid would say, you're a goner!"

Henry paused. There was a part of him that longed to say, "You win, I give in." But there was another part that said: "I've stuck it out so far! Stick it out to the end! Be brave! Be bold! Be a hero! Stand by your right to be as bad as you want to!"

"No one tells me what to do!" cried Henry. "Not you! Not anyone! Not ever! I've told you a hundred times. I'm not telling you again!"

"Please yourself," said Lady Ann. "It's your life. If you don't want it, I'm sure no one else does."

But Henry had a card up his sleeve. There was something Lady Ann had overlooked.

"My mum will have told the police I'm missing! You didn't think of that, did you! They'll have the dogs out looking for me. It'll be in the papers. *And* on telly. The whole country'll be looking for me. I'll be found any minute now! So!" he added defiantly.

"Why should your mum bother about you?" laughed Lady Ann. "She'll be glad to be rid of you. You're a thoroughly unrewarding child."

"Mum doesn't think so!" retorted Henry. "Mum thinks I'm the bees' knees!"

Lady Ann gave a mysterious smile.

"That's what you think Henry, dear!"

"What are you on about?"

"I'll tell you – when I'm ready!" said Lady Ann.

With that, she was gone.

12
Alice

On the day that Henry was kidnapped, Alice had his tea on the table for when he came home from the park. She stood in the kitchen, on the alert, at the ready, ready to open the door the minute he banged it.

She'd spent the afternoon trailing round the shops buying a new jumper for Henry. He'd refused to go with her, saying shopping gave him the pip. But he'd told her the colour that he wanted. He wanted red, pillar box red, and nothing else – or else! For the umpteenth time, she took the jumper out of the bag, and looked at it.

"Oh I do hope Henry likes it," she muttered. "I do so hate it when he's cross."

All her life, she'd tried to be good. She'd tried to be a good little girl, a good teenager, and a specially good wife and mother. She put other people first and always did what they wanted. But then it all went wrong. Henry's dad had walked under a bus.

"And it's all my fault!" sighed Alice.

Why she thought that, only Alice knew, for she'd been at home at the time, cooking his dinner. But there it was, she did think it and guilt gnawed at her like a rat at a bone. She felt sad for herself, that she had no husband. But most of all she felt sad for Henry.

"Poor little fatherless mite!" thought Alice. Henry had no dad, and she must make it up to him. No matter what he did, she mustn't raise her voice, let alone her hand. If he was horrible it was because he was dad-less, which was all her fault in the first place.

"All the same, I sometimes do wish –"

But whatever it was she was about to wish, Alice changed her mind and washed up a dirty cup instead.

"Henry should have been back ten minutes ago. That's odd," she thought. "He's never late for his tea." But since he wasn't there, she'd take the opportunity to have a little rest. After tearing round the shops, she was quite worn out.

Alice went to the sitting room and sat in an armchair. She'd have liked to have put up her aching feet and stretched out on the sofa, but she thought she'd better not get too comfy, Henry would come storming in at any minute.

But minute after minute ticked by.

Still no Henry.

"I expect he's gone to a cricket match, and didn't think to tell me." Alice picked up the newspaper. "I wonder what's on television."

A smile lit up her face. Her favourite gardening man was on! She switched on the programme and watched it to the end.

"I did enjoy that! I haven't watched a programme all the way through for ages. Dear Henry always turns it over or puts his record player on."

She glanced at her watch.

Still no Henry.

"I expect he's gone to a friend's for tea, and now I come to think of it, I'm feeling rather peckish." Humming to herself, she tripped into the kitchen. She got herself cheese on toast of which she was very fond, but which Henry called "Yuk!", together with a buttered scone and black cherry jam and some of the raspberry ripple ice-cream that she'd bought for Henry.

"Something's missing!" thought Alice.

She ran up to her bedroom and fetched a silver vase of violets, then put it on the tray.

"Oh doesn't that look pretty! What fun I'm having! What a treat!" She took the tray into the sitting-room and sank down on the sofa.

When she saw what was on television next, she gave a rapturous squawk of pure delight. It was *Swan Lake*, her favourite ballet. She adored ballet. Now she came to think of it, she'd almost become a ballet dancer herself!

"How strange that I'd forgotten," thought Alice. But it was so long ago, before Henry was even thought of. Before she'd met his dad in fact. But then he'd come along (and oh! how much she missed him!) and they'd got married, and she'd become a Mrs and a mum instead of a ballet dancer.

"Life is a puzzle," sighed Alice. "But I can't think about that now." The orchestra was playing – the ballet had begun.

All too soon, *Swan Lake* was over, and the

dancers were running round the stage, picking up the flowers that the audience had thrown.

"My goodness! How time's flown!" She stretched out like a cat. "What I feel like now is a nice long bath, and a little read in bed."

Still no sight nor sound of Henry.

"I suppose he's staying with his friend, and forgot to tell me," thought Alice.

She made herself a cup of cocoa and drank it, soaking in the bath. Then she climbed into bed and read a gardening book on growing roses. How quiet it was! How peaceful! She gave a gentle yawn, and switched off the light.

"Night, night," she murmured. In two minutes flat she'd fallen fast asleep.

The next morning she woke up with the sun, feeling unusually bright and breezy. She had her breakfast in her dressing-gown, reading the paper.

"I might spend the day in town, then take in a movie. I haven't done that for as long as I can remember. But I suppose," muttered Alice, "I'll have to hurry back for Henry."

Or would she?

"Goodness gracious! Silly me! Henry's spending the week with his friend. I'm sure I remember him telling me. How could I have forgotten?"

So she went to town and saw a movie, then had dinner in a restaurant. The next day, she went to the gardening centre and bought herself lots of plants and rose bushes and set to planting them in her garden.

"Now I come to think of it Henry said he'd be away for two weeks, not one. I hope he's having a nice time with his friend," said Alice.

Then she went and fetched a spade to do some mulching for her roses.

I wrote down "mulching for her roses" and waited for Lady Ann to go on.

"What are you waiting for, Jemima?" she asked. "That's the end of the chapter."

"But it can't be!" I cried.

"Why not, might I ask?"

"This chapter's all about Alice. What happened after she'd mulched her roses? What happened when she went to the police about Henry?"

"She didn't *go* to the police. After she'd mulched her roses, she had a bath and went to the opera."

"What!" I gasped, in stunned amazement. "But what about Henry? Alice knew he wasn't staying with a friend. She just made that up so she could do what she wanted! You said she was always good! You said she always put other people first! You said . . ."

"For goodness sake stop shouting, Jemima! You're beginning to sound like Henry!"

The very thought of me being like Henry was enough to make me shut my mouth. But inside I was seething and, Lady Ann being Lady Ann, she knew it.

"I don't know why you're getting in such a temper. Not long ago you were all for Henry getting his comeuppance."

"Well, yes, I was," I said. "But I can tell you this," I added, "*my* mother wouldn't go lying to herself like that."

Lady Ann just raised an eyebrow and smiled.

"I'll prove it," I said.

The next morning at breakfast I came straight out with it: "Do you tell lies?" I asked my mother.

"I try not to," she replied.

"Do you tell secret lies to yourself?" I pressed.

My mother sighed. "Again, I try not to. But sometimes, maybe I do."

"Oh," I said. "Look," I went on, "if I was kidnapped, would you pretend to yourself I was staying with a friend?"

My mother's face filled with laughter. "Of course not, darling. What an extraordinary idea! Whatever made you ask?"

"Nothing," I said. "I just wondered."

Poor Henry, I thought, left all to himself in his dark hour of need.

I was sorry for him. Maybe I shouldn't have been. But I was. I admit it.

13
Do or Die

Henry leant back against the belfry wall and inspected his arms and legs. "They've got thinner than sticks," he muttered. "Soon I'll be a weed like Simon Beavers."

Hunger gnawed at his belly and thirst scratched at his throat. He'd had nothing to eat for 200 hours. Not that he knew how long it had been. He'd lost all sense of time. Days and nights merged into each other. Henry sighed. He felt he'd been in the belfry for ever.

When Lady Ann had left him, he'd been full of bold thoughts. He wasn't going to let her get the better of him. And he wasn't going to give in to despair either. He'd tried that before and it only made him feel worse. He'd exercise and keep himself fit instead. Then when they found him everyone would be amazed at what good shape he was in and how brave he'd been.

"I'll be a hero!" thought Henry.

Even when he didn't feel like it, he forced himself to do press-ups and jog round the belfry to stop his body getting stiff. To keep his mind alert, he learnt every word on the biscuit packets and Coke tins and practised saying them faster and faster without pausing for breath.

But as the days passed, Henry found himself getting weaker and fainter, and he gave up his exercises. He kept dozing off and his dreams were always about food: plates of sausages and chips, whopping big hamburgers dripping with ketchup, hot crispy rolls oozing butter, huge cartons of raspberry ripple ice-cream and mountains of his biggest food favourite, chocolate cake.

Henry wrapped the blanket tighter round him. It was going to be a cold night. It had been raining most of the day. This had been a good thing in one way, however: he'd been able to collect some rainwater in a Coke tin, which had helped to quench his raging thirst.

For this he was grateful. In his situation, he was grateful for small mercies.

"Come on Alfred, up you come!" said Henry. He picked up the rat which was cleaning its whiskers on the floor beside him. "Come under the blanket with me. It's warmer."

The rat took up Henry's offer, and nestled in his lap. Henry stroked him. "We're mates, you and me, aren't we? I was silly to be scared of you. You're not horrible like people say. They've got it all wrong about you, and the bats. And when I get out of here I'm going to tell everyone – that's a promise!"

Henry leant back. He wished he didn't feel so weak. He wished his head would stop spinning. His eyelids started to close. Then they suddenly jerked open.

"Lady Ann!"

"Hullo, Henry. My oh my! We are looking a little pale around the gills, aren't we!"

At the sight of Lady Ann, Henry's fighting spirit returned.

"I feel fine!" he retorted. "I feel great."

"You won't feel so great when I tell you

141

what I've got to tell you!" said Lady Ann.

She didn't try to soften the blow. She dropped the bombshell direct. She told Henry that his mum hadn't reported him missing. "Your mother has told herself you're staying with a friend," concluded Lady Ann.

"But she can't have! I haven't got a friend. I've never had a friend. Mum knows that. She wouldn't just forget me!"

"I don't see why not!"

"Because I'm her son!"

"You're a dreadful son. The best thing any mother could do is forget you!"

"Mum'd never do anything so wicked!"

"Oh and who's talking! You're a little saint I suppose!"

"That's different!" raged Henry. "You know it is!"

"Why?" queried Lady Ann.

"Don't you start all that 'why' stuff again!" cried Henry.

All sorts of feelings were racing round inside him. He was furious with his mum. He was hurt. But most of all he was astonished.

"You're making this up!" he screeched as loudly as his parched-dry throat would allow. "Even if my mum wanted to forget me – which she wouldn't, she'd never dare!"

"Well, it seems she has dared, Henry dear, and it's no more than you deserve!" grinned Lady Ann. "Why should your mother care about you? Did you care two hoots about her? You don't even know what she looks like!"

"I do!" protested Henry.

"What colour hair has she got?"

"Er . . . brown."

"Wrong. Blonde. What colour eyes?"

"Brown!"

"Wrong again. Blue. Is she fat or thin?"

"Thin?" ventured Henry.

"Neither fat nor thin," said Lady Ann. "Is she small or tall?"

"Neither small nor tall."

"Clever, Henry. But wrong. Your mother is most definitely tall. I know what your mother looks like better than you do. I also know you made her life a misery. You treated her like a doormat."

"But she didn't mind being a doormat! She

143

liked being a doormat! She was used to it!" cried Henry.

"Huh! What would you know? You don't know what your mother's like on the outside, let alone inside. You never gave her a thought in all your ghastly little life."

"Shut up! I'm fed up with listening to you!"

But Lady Ann, it seemed, was in a talkative mood, and determined to milk her moment of triumph.

"I must say," she went on with a gloating smile, "your mother has more sense than I gave her credit for. I thought she'd put up with you for ever. But it seems the worm has turned. Three cheers for Alice! Good for her, say I!"

Henry put out his tongue, and turned his back on Lady Ann. He didn't want her to see the tears he felt rising to his eyes. He knew he'd never bothered much about his mum. What was the point? She'd never notice anyway. She was always lost in a world of her own. Even when she was doing things for him, her mind seemed to be a million miles away, as if she was an alien who'd just dropped by from another planet. It didn't matter how horrible he was, or how much he shouted and bossed her around, she didn't take it in. It just went through her, as if she was a ghost, like Lady Ann. Well, not like Lady Ann – *her* beady eyes noticed every little thing.

"I don't care!" he cried. "I don't care about you or Mum or anyone! And if you think I'm coming crawling to you, you evil old bat, I'm not! I'd rather die!"

"Good," said Lady Ann. "Because that is what you're going to do. You won't last much longer. A few more days and you'll be ghostified like me."

Henry felt a stab of fear. But he wasn't letting on to Lady Ann, and he put on his boldest face.

"I wouldn't mind being ghostified," he said. "As a matter of fact I'd *like* it! I could haunt people and play tricks on them. I could walk through walls. I could get to any place in the world, just by thinking about it, like you do. I'd never get tired. I'd never get sick. I could eat 500 chocolate cakes a day without puking. *And* I wouldn't have to pay for them. I could just nick them from a shop and no one could stop me—"

Henry broke off. Lady Ann was laughing as if she'd never stop.

"What's so funny!" he demanded.

"Ghosts don't eat, you silly boy!" cried Lady Ann.

"What!" squeaked Henry.

"Ghosts don't eat food, you foolish child. They don't need it. Look at me, I'm pure energy as it is. Besides, where would I put it? I've no body to put it in."

"You mean you don't eat *anything*!" Henry, already pale, turned even paler.

"Not a sausage!" said Lady Ann.

"What, never!"

"No, Henry. Not ever."

"Oh," whispered Henry.

He hadn't really been too keen on being a ghost in the first place. Now he'd quite definitely gone off the idea. No food! Never again to crunch his way through a packet of crisps, lick an ice-cream, suck a toffee. Never again to munch on a hot-dog or chomp a hamburger.

Never, in all eternity, to eat chocolate cake again! "I'm too young for that! I'm too young not to have chocolate cake!"

"You should have thought of that before," retorted Lady Ann. "Now, I've no more time to waste. I won't see you again in the flesh. I shall do my best to avoid you as a ghost. In my experience, those who are revolting as humans are just as revolting as ghosts. Farewell, Henry."

She began to vanish.

"Wait! Please!" cried Henry.

At the word "please", Lady Ann stopped halfway through the wall.

"Well?" she demanded.

"I'll do a deal, Lady Ann," he mumbled.

"What sort of deal?" asked Lady Ann.

Henry paused and swallowed. He swallowed his pride. He ate his words. Not because he was afraid of dying, though he was, just a little. Not because he repented of his bad ways. But because he couldn't bear never to have chocolate cake again.

"If you'll help me out of here, I'll er . . .

mend my ways. I can't promise to be perfect. But I'll be as good as I can instead of as bad as I can."

Lady Ann looked at Henry.

"Are you sure about this?"

Slowly, Henry nodded.

Lady Ann pondered. She looked at Henry for a long, long time.

"Very well," she said at last. "I'll see what I can do."

"I'm most grateful, Lady Ann."

As he spoke, something most peculiar happened. Henry felt a great surge of happiness rise up inside him.

He grinned at Lady Ann.

"You didn't really win, you know! I always wanted to be good anyway. So!"

A smile flitted over his face. Then Henry gave a little moan and fell in a heap upon the floor.

"He's dead! Oh no! Oh Henry!" Lady Ann stood aghast. A lump rose to her throat. To lose him now, just when he was going to be good and be the kind of grandson she'd always longed for. Of course, she could meet

him as a ghost. But a ghost wasn't quite the same as a flesh and blood boy.

"It's not fair!" she cried. "It's just not fair."

She hadn't said that since she'd lost her head. Full of grief, she bent over Henry. She saw his chest rise and fall. There was still some breath left in him. But time was running out.

"He's at death's door! He's almost a corpse! I must act at once."

Then an awful thought dawned. She remembered she was a ghost, and that ghosts couldn't take a life or save one. There'd be too much confusion if one ghost tried to save a person, while another was trying to kill them. So killing people and saving them were both against ghost law.

Lady Ann paced up and down. What should she do? Should she save Henry? Or obey the law?

"Oh Lady Ann," I cried, "what did you do!"

"What did I do? I went for a walk," said Lady Ann. "If I might continue?"

I nodded, fearing the worst for poor Henry. Lady Ann was looking terribly solemn.

"As I was saying, I went for a walk. Through the woods. It just so happened that Ted Topper lived on the other side." Ted, she explained, was a ghost-hunter. And when he saw Lady Ann strolling past his house, he couldn't believe his luck. He pranced around in glee. "Not wanting to be rude," she went on, "you know how I feel about manners, I waved and smiled. Then I went back to see how Henry was getting on. And would you believe it? Ted followed me! All the way up to the belfry—"

"And he found Henry! You saved him after all! Oh, good for you, Lady Ann!"

"I did nothing of the kind!" Lady Ann glowered at me, looking seriously displeased.

"I said not a word to Ted about Henry. Nor did I force Ted to come to the belfry. The choice was his. He came of his own free will, and that's what counts according to the law. It was Ted who saved Henry, I had no part in it. I trust that is clear, Jemima?"

"Er . . . um . . ." I said.

And so it was that Henry was snatched from the jaws of death. But that's not quite the end of the story . . .

14
Lady Ann and Me

"Is there any R.R.?" I asked Dad one afternoon when I got back from school. It was a
sweltering day and I was boiling hot.

"Yes," said Dad. "I thought you might want
some R.R. today. So I got some specially for
you."

R.R. is our code name for raspberry ripple
ice-cream which is my absolute favourite.

"Dear old Dad," I thought. "He really is a
sweetie."

My Dad's a solicitor. He works from home,
sorting out people's wills and divorces, nothing very thrilling. Frankly there's nothing very
thrilling about Dad. He's the sort of person
who disappears in a crowd. You can be in a
room for half an hour before you even notice
he's there.

My mum – now, that's a different matter!
My Mum's stage name is Belinda Bean – yes,

the Belinda Bean. She's been in more films than I can remember and is incredibly famous. She's also incredibly beautiful and incredibly nice. People who tell you you can't be clever and beautiful *and* nice have got it wrong. My mum's the living proof.

When she can, Mum takes me filming with her. When she can't, I stay home with dear old Dad.

Dad has a heart of gold. He always remembers to buy me R.R. and things like that. It's not his fault he's so ordinary and not specially good at anything. Though last week he told me something which surprised me:

"When I was your age, Jemima," he said, "I was a brain-box. Top of my class in everything."

He saw I didn't believe him.

"Yes," he went on, "I was a real whizz kid."

"What went wrong, Dad?" I asked.

Dad laughed. "Nothing," he said. "But when I grew up and went out into the world, I found there were lots of whizz kids like me. All the girls and boys who'd come top of their schools. There were hundreds and thousands of us. I was just one of a very large crowd."

I didn't know what to say to that.

"The funny thing is," said Dad, "that the chap who was a real no-no, always bottom of the class, became quite remarkably brilliant."

Dad took a few puffs of his pipe and scratched the bald patch at the back of his head.

"Yes," he went on, "I was reading about this chap only a few days ago. He's heading a new mission into space and is tipped for the Nobel prize. Life's a funny old thing, my pet."

Well, I had to agree if life could turn a whizz kid into a dull old stick like my Dad, it was very odd indeed!

I went indoors to get my R.R. I was just getting a bowl out to put it in when I suddenly went all cold. An icy blast went down my spine. And there before me stood a ghost with a neck but no head.

My knees went weak. My legs gave way. I fell – *flop*! on to the floor.

"Get up, you silly girl. I'm not going to hurt you!"

That was my first meeting with Lady Ann.

She inspected me from head to toe from the head tucked underneath her arm. It was a very strange experience.

"Don't droop, girl! Shoulders back! Head up! That's better." She eyed me carefully. "Yes, there's certainly the look of Henry about you."

And that was the first I heard of Henry.

"Who's Henry?" I asked.

"A boy who gave me a great deal of trouble. It's a long story, Jemima, and I want you to write it down for me."

I started that night and kept on going every night after that till we got up to Henry's rescue.

"And did Henry keep his promise? Did he mend his wicked ways?"

"Indeed he did," said Lady Ann.

"And what about Alice? Did Henry forgive her? Not that I'd blame him if he didn't!"

"They forgave each other. Alice, however, felt her mind was in a muddle–"

"I should think it was!" I said. "Forgetting her very own son, accidentally on purpose!"

"Be that as it may, Alice took herself to a

155

mind doctor to get it sorted out. I just wish we'd had mind doctors in my day! I'd have sent Albert to see one like a shot. Hiding his own gold, then blaming me for it! If anyone's mind was in a mess, it was his!"

She was about to say something else, when my dad walked in. I picked up a book and pretended to read.

"I saw your light was on, Jemima. And I thought I heard voices." Then he gave a cry. "Good grief, it's Lady Ann."

"Hullo, Henry dear. You're looking very well. If just a trifle fat!"

"You know me, Lady Ann. Always a greedy guts!" He turned to me. "I see you've met my daughter."

I just looked at him. My eyes were popping. My mouth had dropped almost to the floor.

"I've been telling her our story, Henry dear," said Lady Ann.

"Have you indeed? It's quite a story, eh Jemima?"

"But Dad," I stuttered, "you're n-not! You c-can't be H-H-H-Horrible Henry!"

"I'm afraid so," he said.

"But your name is James!"

"James is my second name. I dropped 'Henry' when I turned over a new leaf. I did a good job of it, wouldn't you say?"

I didn't say anything. I couldn't. I just gawped. Another astonishing thought was slowly dawning. If Dad was Horrible Henry, then . . .

"Gran must be Alice!" I gibbered. "But Gran's nothing like Alice . . ."

Except for one thing! Alice liked gardening! So does my Gran! In fact, Gran owns a market garden, a huge one, with lots of people working for her. She's terribly nice, but just a little bit awesome.

"I wasn't the only one who turned over a new leaf!" chuckled Dad.

"I knew my grandson's mother must be a woman of distinction. I always had faith in Alice," crowed Lady Ann.

The two of them stood there, looking immensely pleased with themselves. Not a thought for me! Never mind that I was shattered, in a state of total shock:

Horrible Henry = my Dad

Drippy Alice = my Gran

And my grandmother thirty-one times removed was a headless ghost! No wonder I was reeling.

"Well, I think that brings me to the end of the story. All that remains," said Lady Ann, pointing to the exercise books piled up on my bed, "is to get them made into a proper book!"

"But you can't do that!" I shrieked, as if suddenly stung. "People would read it! They'd know my dad was Horrible Henry!"

"So what!" said Lady Ann.

"It wouldn't be fair," I explained. "It wouldn't be fair to Dad. He's very sensitive you know!"

Lady Ann turned on me. She was positively bristling. "I trust you're not arguing, Jemima! Remember I'm your grandmother thirty-one times removed!"

Was I likely to forget!

"I'm not arguing," I muttered. "I was just thinking of Dad."

"Your father can think for himself. And he thinks it's a splendid idea. In fact," she went on, giving Dad her oh-so-sweet smile, "you can do the drawings, Henry dear."

And would you believe it, Dad did!

Which is all there is to tell.

So goodbye for now from
Lady Ann
Horrible Henry
and me.
Yours sincerely,
Jemima Bunberry.